The Ground Hog Mystery

Annette Vetter Adventure #6

February 1969

by Ann Carol Ulrich

The Ground Hog Mystery

Ann Carol Ulrich

Earth Star Publications
P.O. Box 1213
Cedaredge, CO 81413

FIRST EDITION
First Printing July 2016
Second Printing January 2017

ISBN 978-0-944851-45-6

Printed in the United States of America

Other Annette Vetter Books

The Mystery at Hickory Hill
Annette Vetter Adventure #1

The Secret of the Green Paint
Annette Vetter Adventure #2

The Pouting Pumpkin Mystery
Annette Vetter Adventure #3

The Legend of the Lantern
Annette Vetter Adventure #4

In the Shadow of the Tower
Annette Vetter Adventure #5

Other Young Adult Books

By Ann Carol Ulrich

The Root Cellar Mystery

Acknowledgments

I wish to thank all you readers who have been a part of Annette's life. She has come a long way since 1968, and what a pleasure it has been to have her share her adolescence with me all these years, even though I no longer reside in Wisconsin.

Many times I have said that she's the girl who lives the life I fantasized—growing up on a farm with animals, surrounded by the woods and nature, with a best friend, a collie to keep her company while her mom works nights—and discovering the world of boys, in particular *one* she hoped she would end up with someday.

Thank you, Doug, for helping me understand what it was like during the Vietnam conflict, and for the meaningful conversations we had about that war and those who were unfortunate enough to be Missing in Action. Also thanks to my brother Jim, for further advice about the Vietnam scenes. Both of your service to our country made us all safer, and I am proud that you are both part of my life.

Special thanks to my niece, Sharon Hunter, an author in her own right, who turned me on to NANOWRIMO (National Novel Writers Month) and got me inspired to write not only this book, but the one before it, and the one that follows ... which I can't *wait* to begin.

Ann Carol Ulrich (Miller)

To Jessica "Clyde"

You still warm my heart

Contents

The
Ground Hog
Mystery

ACU

1

A Special Card

In the woods, everything was new and green. Annette had been sitting on a patch of grass beside a stream, watching a pair of robins building a nest in a small tree close by. She stretched back and stared up at the blue sky as fluffy white clouds slowly floated by as in a sea. A warm breeze tousled her auburn hair and she could feel the caress of sunshine on her bare feet.

Glancing to her right, she saw someone walking toward her out of the thick brush. Shielding her eyes, she watched him grin as he leisurely made his way toward her. His hand casually swept the lock of dark hair off his forehead and his green eyes made her heart skip a beat.

"I thought I'd find you here," said Tim Duncan. He crouched toward her and she sat up, reaching out her hand. He gently pulled Annette to her feet and they faced one another, smiling. She waited breathlessly as he drew even nearer, and then he wrapped her in his arms and held her in a tight embrace.

Rrr-r-r-r-r-r-ringgggg!!

The sound the alarm clock beside the bed pulled Annette out of her warm dream and her eyes opened to the dark bedroom upstairs in the Vetter farmhouse. She reached over and immediately shut off the alarm, then sank back against her pillow and pulled the blanket around her for warmth.

Annette knew she had to get up, get into her milking clothes, and go out to the barn to do her chores before it was time to get ready for school. She usually didn't have any problem getting out of bed, even on the coldest winter mornings, but *this* morning the dream only made her want to go back to sleep and see what happened next … with *Tim*.

She almost did lapse back into slumber, but then her collie, Ginger, nosed her cheek. Annette's blue eyes opened and she patted the dog's white mane and watched his red swishy tail move back and forth as he told her in his own way that the cows were waiting.

Silently, Annette got out of bed without waking Ruby, and gathered her clothes to take to the bathroom. Everyone else in the house was still asleep—Mrs. Vetter in the front upstairs bedroom, and Annette's brother Terry, who slept in the room next to the girls.

After she was through in the bathroom, Annette made her way downstairs with Ginger at her side. The light of day was visible from the kitchen window as she opened the refrigerator and took out the orange juice. After downing a small glass, she pulled on her boots and farm coat, and then went outside to the barn, where her Holsteins, Elizabeth and Alice, were waiting to get milked.

Ginger shook himself, then lay down in a pile of hay while Annette grabbed her gear from the storage room and pulled the milking stool up beside Alice, who was giving an abundance of milk now that she had given birth to the calf on Christmas Eve. She recalled how Mr. Duncan, Penny's and Tim's father, had taken the little bullock they had named Donovan, to the Duncan farm a week later.

Elizabeth waited patiently while her sister got milked. Annette could see that Elizabeth was starting to show a little. Her calf would be born in May, according to Mr. Duncan and Doctor Slater, the veterinarian. She always used milking time to go over her thoughts, and today her thoughts were focused on Tim Duncan.

"I wish it *were* spring," Annette mumbled. Ginger's collie ears perked up at the sound of her voice and his brown eyes stared at her as her fingers worked at extracting the milk from Alice's udder.

She shivered a bit and tried not to think about the fact that it was only the end of January and there were still two long months of winter ahead in west central Wisconsin.

After Christmas, Mrs. Vetter had gone to the county courthouse and applied for custody of Terry and his sister, Ruby Foley, who were—for all intents and purposes— orphans. Their mother had committed suicide in Colorado Springs just after Thanksgiving, and Ruby's father—Terry's stepfather—was "Missing in Action" in Vietnam. They presumed Bob Foley was dead, but this, Annette knew, had not yet been confirmed.

She recalled how everything had played out last month, when Terry had come to Ravensville because he had discovered, after his mother's death, that Annette's father, Tom Vetter, had been his dad. Annette had found out that her father had been married before he met her mother, and unknown to all of them, Terry's mother had been pregnant with him when she got the annulment. It had been a shock to Mrs. Vetter, Annette realized, but it had been a happy moment for Annette when she learned that she had a half-brother.

Of course, it was due to all the trouble in Colorado Springs that Terry had escaped with his sister Ruby, who had been molested at her foster home. The two kids had taken the Greyhound bus to Madison, where their Uncle Will Knutson lived and had agreed to help them. Now Uncle Will was becoming a regular visitor, driving up from Madison about every two weeks to spend an overnight visit with his niece and nephew.

Annette finished up her work, then went with Ginger to the chicken house to collect the eggs and feed the flock. Egg production was just starting to increase a little, she noticed, as the days were now getting longer and the chickens were just as anxious as she was to experience warmer weather.

Mrs. Vetter and Terry were already up and in the kitchen, getting their coffee, when Annette walked into the house with her basket of eggs. She removed her boots, which had just a trace of snow and ice on them, and hung her farm coat up on one of the hooks behind the door.

"Well, good morning." Mrs. Vetter smiled at her daughter.

"Hi, Mom. Hi, Terry." Annette grinned.

The tall blond boy smiled back and reached for the cream pitcher on the kitchen counter. "Good morning, Annette," he said. "I think I heard Ruby rustling around upstairs."

"Would you like some bacon and eggs this morning?" asked Mrs. Vetter. She had already gotten dressed and was pulling a frying pan out from one of the lower kitchen cupboards.

"Sure," said Annette, "that sounds great."

"Let me help," said Terry. "I think I saw some cheese in the fridge. Do you mind if I make us omelets?"

Mrs. Vetter laughed and picked up her coffee cup. "I can't get used to this new life. You're spoiling me."

"No such thing," said Annette. "Mom, both our lives have changed since Terry and Ruby came to live with us. I love having you home more … and especially in the evenings."

Mrs. Vetter chuckled. "Well, I've got a family to watch over now," she replied.

Annette thought she had never seen her mother look as

happy as she did, now that she had switched to part-time at
the hospital and was going in only three full shifts a week. Mrs.
Vetter had decided that if she was going to adopt Terry and
Ruby, she needed to be home for them all as much as she could
while still keeping her nursing job at Ravensville General.

Annette pulled out Ginger's kibble and was filling his
dish when they heard footsteps coming down the stairs. A
moment later, Ruby appeared, wearing a blue, long-sleeved
dress for school, her blonde hair brushed into two pigtails.

"Did I hear Terry say we're having omelets?" The 13-
year-old petted Ginger, who had come over to greet her before
Annette set his dish down on the floor.

"You look lovely this morning, Ruby," said Mrs. Vetter.

"Thank you." The girl lowered her blue eyes and humbly
walked over to the kitchen table to sit down.

"How did you sleep?" asked Terry.

"Fine," said Ruby.

"No bad dreams?"

"Well …" The girl looked at her brother and shrugged. "A
few, maybe."

Annette sighed. "No nightmares, at least … right, Ruby?"

Ruby smiled up at her, then looked away.

Annette secretly smiled to herself as she poured a cup of
coffee and let herself fall back into the memory of Tim's touch
in her dream upon waking. Then she remembered something.
"Oh, I don't want to forget …"

"What is it?" asked Ruby.

Annette rushed to the stairs and ran up to her bedroom
that she and Ruby shared, where she had left a large envelope
on her desk. She picked it up and placed it next to her purse
and her homework, then quickly changed into her school
clothes.

The smell of bacon wafted up from the kitchen when she
was in the bathroom, washing up and putting on her makeup.

Before going back downstairs, she went to her room and pulled out the card she had made. Her heart began to beat faster as she read through it, then placed it back into its sleeve. She prayed she had chosen her words carefully and would not have any regrets.

At seven o'clock, after they had eaten, Annette and Terry bundled up in their winter coats just as Annette looked out the window and saw Penny, wearing her winter coat and boots, walking up the driveway. When they stepped out the door onto the porch, Ginger barked his greeting and ran through the snowy path to where the dark-haired girl with green eyes waved at them.

"Morning!" called Penny.

"Have a good day," Ruby called out as Annette and Terry left the house. They had plenty of time this morning to make the rural bus that went to Ravensville's high school. Ruby's bus came half an hour later and stopped at the Vetters' driveway to pick her up and take her to the junior high school.

Since early January, after the Christmas vacation was over, Terry accompanied Annette and Penny to the bus stop every morning, except on those days when Penny's brother Tim gave them a ride. He usually helped Mr. Duncan finish the milking at their dairy farm and sometimes got to school a little later.

"I'm getting so tired of winter," Annette said as they walked along the side of the icy pavement on Ogden Road. "I had a dream last night that it was spring." She secretly smiled as the vision of Tim bending toward her replayed in her mind.

"Oh, me too," agreed Penny. "We've had more snow this year than I can remember." She looked over at Annette's brother. "Terry, how do Wisconsin winters compare to what it's like in Colorado Springs?"

Annette's tall blond brother walked on the inner edge of the highway. "Well, as far as I can see … winter is winter, no matter where you live. We could get some pretty nasty blizzards on the Front Range, you know."

"That means the Denver and Colorado Springs side of the Rocky Mountains," explained Annette.

"Just think," said Penny, panting a little as she tried to keep up with the other two. "Mandy Mitchell lives near Gunnison, and I heard that's the coldest town in Colorado. It gets way below zero sometimes."

Terry laughed and a cloud of air puffed from his mouth. "Some say Alamosa is worse yet."

"Where's that?" asked Annette.

"It's in the San Luis Valley," said Terry, and he began telling the girls what he knew about the parts of Colorado he had seen when he lived in that state, which had actually only been three or four years.

When they finally reached the bus stop, a few other kids had gathered from nearby homes, and within a couple of minutes, the big yellow school bus rolled into view and its wheels squealed as it came to a stop at the corner of Ogden Road and Tower Drive.

Penny climbed on before Annette and Terry, and walked straight to the back of the bus, where she saw Pete Randt watching them with a grin on his face. He swept a lock of dark hair off his forehead.

"Hi, Pete," called Annette with a smile. She followed Penny, who swung into the empty seat in front of Pete. Terry brushed past and sat next to Pete as he moved over to make room.

"How's it goin'?" Terry greeted him.

"Not so bad." Pete leaned over the girls' seat. "Hey, Annette, did you get that Geometry assignment?"

She turned her head and made a face at him. "Yeah …"

"I couldn't figure out that last problem."

"I hate math," grumbled Penny as the bus started rolling

down the road.

Annette laughed at her friend. "You're an A student!"

"So? That doesn't mean I have to like it."

"Want me to look at your homework?" Terry offered.

Pete made a face. "Well ..."

Penny spun around and grabbed Pete's books. "Here, let me see." She opened his Geometry book and turned to the bookmarked page.

With a big smile, Pete leaned over the seat and then handed Penny his notebook containing the assignment.

"What part didn't you understand?"

"Pete ..." said Annette. She stood up in the aisle of the bus. "Sit down. I'll sit next to my brother."

Pete immediately changed places with her and Annette swung into the back seat of the bus beside Terry.

"Did Ruby have any more bad dreams?" he asked in a low voice while Penny and Pete were consulting about his math homework.

Annette glanced up at the concerned look in her brother's blue eyes. "I don't think so. Not last night, at least," she said.

"I'm glad," he replied.

"Me too," said Annette. Ruby had started having nightmares about a week after New Year's. Since she and Annette shared the bedroom, Annette had been rudely awakened about six or seven times since then, with Ruby crying out in her sleep, sometimes kicking, sometimes waving her arms, and Annette had tried her best to calm the girl, who would then cry herself to sleep.

"She's been through a lot in the last coupl'a months," said Terry, still keeping his voice low.

"Yes, I know," said Annette. "But when she's awake during the day, she seems cheerful and happy."

"That's her nature." Terry smiled to himself. "My little sister is always looking on the bright side of things. She's the one you want to be with when you're feeling down."

As they rounded a corner, the books shifted on Annette's lap and she had to grab hold before she lost her grip. As a result, her purse came loose and fell on the floor of the aisle. Terry reached down to retrieve it from her and as he pulled the purse up, the large white envelope fell out.

Pete noticed it and reached for it. Before he gave it back to Annette, he turned it over and read what she'd written on the front in big letters: HAPPY BIRTHDAY, TIM

"What's this?" he asked.

Penny immediately snatched the envelope from Pete's hands and laughed out loud. "Annette, did you get that bum brother of mine a birthday card?"

Annette blushed as other kids on the bus turned and stared at her.

"Oh, is it Tim's birthday?" asked Terry.

Annette grew embarrassed and started rearranging the books on her lap. "Uh… well…"

"Today is January 30th," said Penny. "Yup, it's Tim's birthday."

"Did you forget?" Pete asked her.

"No way could I forget," said Penny. "He's eighteen today. Do you think Tim would let anyone forget that he's turning eighteen?"

"Wow," breathed Pete. "That means …"

"He's an adult! Or so he thinks." Penny giggled.

Annette reached for the envelope, but Penny held it away from her and turned it around to examine it.

"I wonder what's inside this card," she said.

"Give it back," Annette demanded.

"Oh, I will," said Penny.

"It must be very… personal," said Pete, who turned and gave Annette a sympathetic smile.

"Hey, when's your birthday, Terry?" Penny turned

around to face him.

"March 18th," he disclosed. "When's yours?"

Penny sighed as she handed the envelope to Pete, who looked at the fancy script on front, then reluctantly gave it back to Annette. "May 6th is my birthday. I could have had my driver's learning permit in November, but I decided to wait until Annette gets hers next month."

"Are you getting your learner's permit soon?" asked Pete, his brown eyes wide.

Annette stuffed the birthday card deep into her purse and zipped it shut. "On the 11th of February," she disclosed. "I'll be fifteen and a half. Pen and I are going down to the DMV that day to take our tests."

"I can't wait!" Penny had finished helping Pete with his math problem and handed his notebook back to him. Turning around to face Annette and her brother, her green eyes widened. "Then you and Tim can teach Annette and me how to drive!"

Terry laughed softly. "I'm not yet eighteen. I'm not even seventeen … not until March, that is."

Pete cleared his throat and grumbled. "Heck … I won't get my learner's permit until the end of April."

"You probably can," said Terry. "Some states let farm kids get their permits when they're younger."

"Hey, yeah …" Penny grinned at Pete, who smiled sheepishly.

"I hate being younger than everybody else," he said.

"Nonsense," said Annette. She pulled the lipstick out of her purse and touched up her mouth. Then she felt relieved that no one said anything more about the birthday card she was going to give to Tim.

2

In a Quandary

Annette came out of the women's bathroom after lunch in the school cafeteria. She looked up and down the hallway. It was still five minutes before the bell for fifth hour classes. Students were lingering at their lockers, talking and visiting, or wandering in one direction or another.

Before heading to the sophomore hallway, where she shared her locker with Penny, Annette held her purse close against her chest and ventured down the hall toward the senior lockers. Lisa Kowalski, a senior girl who was president of Future Farmers of America, saw Annette and called out, "Annette, how are you doing?"

Annette stopped and smiled at the tall, dark-haired girl with glasses. "Great," she said and kept looking down the hallway.

"One of the soldiers wrote me a long letter," said Lisa. "I guess our cookie project last month was a success."

Annette knew Lisa was referring to the FFA project in which she and Penny had helped bake Christmas treats to send to some troops serving in Vietnam. "Oh, that's cool," said Annette.

"His name is Gary and he's a corporal," said Lisa. "Hey,

are you looking for someone?"

Annette felt her face redden. "Uh … actually, just Tim," she revealed. "I have something for him."

"Tim Duncan?"

Annette nodded, and then Patty Morris, Lisa's locker mate, stood up after retrieving some books. "I saw Tim in the Resource Center," she said. "I was just there and Mr. Edwards was helping him with some information on colleges."

Annette sighed. "I guess I'll catch him later. The bell's about to ring." With a quick smile, she headed back toward the sophomore lockers. She was passing through the junior hallway when she noticed her brother Terry, standing with two junior girls who practically had him trapped as they flirted, obviously competing for the boy's attention. He noticed Annette and waved with a soft-spoken smile.

She giggled as she approached Penny at their locker. Terry, she knew, was the latest hot item at Ravensville High. Kathy Evans and Debbie Kelton were at the locker and greeted Annette.

"Where did you go?" Penny demanded.

"I was looking for Tim," Annette confessed, "but apparently he's in the Resource Center."

Debbie pretended to swoon at the mention of Tim's name. Kathy poked Debbie with her elbow and smirked. "There you go again."

"Where is he applying for college?" asked Debbie.

"To heck if I know." Penny bent down and started rooting through the papers in the bottom of their locker. "Oh no, where's my English paper? Annette, have you seen it?"

"Not likely," said Annette, eyeing the mess.

Kathy crossed her arms and leaned over. "Annette, that brother of yours is all the rage."

Debbie squealed and squinted her eyes. "Ooh … Terry is so cute."

Kathy's brown eyes expanded. "Annette, are you asking Pete Randt to the Valentines Dance this year?"

"The Valentines Dance? When is it?" asked Annette.

"Silly question," said Debbie. "It's on Valentines Day, of course."

"Well, are you?" pressed Kathy.

Penny's head bobbed up and she looked hopefully at Annette, waiting for her to answer.

"Uh ..." Annette swallowed. "I don't know yet. Pen, hurry up. The bell's gonna ring any minute."

Kathy jerked around. "Oh, gosh, you're right. Come on, Deb."

"See ya later." Debbie followed Kathy down the hall while Annette waited to retrieve her books for afternoon classes.

Annette fretted all afternoon about giving Tim his birthday card. She hadn't seen anything of him all day, which really wasn't that unusual, except that she wanted to be sure she gave him the card in person.

At the end of seventh hour, five minutes before the bell rang, the intercom came on and Mr. Edwards, the assistant principal, gave the announcements.

"The Valentines Dance is going to be held on Friday, the 14th," he said over the loudspeaker. "This is a 'girls ask boys' affair, but girls must first purchase a hunting license, which will be available at the front office starting tomorrow morning."

Some snickers erupted in the Geometry class. Annette noticed Pete looking in her direction and she smiled. She gathered her things together while Mr. Edwards finished with some other brief announcements, and then the bell rang and everyone got up to leave the room.

Out in the hallway, Annette made a beeline for the senior wing. She figured she would have just enough time to find Tim, hand him the card, and get back to her locker so that she and Penny could catch the bus. She worried that he would be surrounded by his usual adoring girlfriends, and she wouldn't be able to get a word in edgewise. By the time she reached that end of the school, her heart was pounding from anticipation.

"Annette!"

She spun around and it felt as though her heart had taken a flying leap. "Tim! There you are."

His green eyes met hers with a warm smile and he squeezed her arm affectionately. Before he could respond, she thrust the large white envelope into his hand. "Happy birthday." She grinned up at him.

"Oh … wow," said Tim, turning the envelope over and reading her script. "Gosh, thanks, Annette."

"Don't … don't open it yet," she said hastily. "Wait till you get home." Then, terribly embarrassed, she smiled once more, then darted down the hall to get her coat.

Pete was standing at their locker, talking to Penny when Annette came rushing up to them.

"Why are you out of breath?" asked Penny.

Pete chuckled as Annette grabbed her coat and her boots, scarf and mittens. She didn't answer her friend.

"Come on, we're gonna miss the bus." Penny led the way toward the door as they followed.

Mrs. Vetter was home when the school bus delivered Ruby to the end of their driveway. She watched as the girl made her way to the house, practically skipping up the snowy driveway. She let Ginger out the door and the collie ran down the porch steps to greet his new friend.

"Well, how was school today?"

Ruby grinned and climbed the steps to the porch. Mrs. Vetter held the kitchen door open for her as she entered, followed by an ecstatic collie. "Guess what, Mom? Miss Graves gave me an A on my book report."

"Well, good for you, Ruby," said Mrs. Vetter.

"And can I go over to Kay Randt's house tomorrow after school?"

"Oh … you mean Peter's sister?"

"Yes, she's in seventh grade, but we're good friends," said Ruby. "Then maybe sometime I can have Kay come over here."

"Why, that sounds fine with me," said Mrs. Vetter. "I do have to work tomorrow, so someone would have to drive you home."

"I'll check with Kay on that." Ruby removed her coat and set her books down on the kitchen table. "Oh, did you know that the Randts' barn cat just had kittens?"

Mrs. Vetter chuckled as she went to the refrigerator and took out a plate of brownies she had made earlier. "How about a brownie and a glass of milk?"

"Oh!" Ruby's face lit up. Then she asked, "How come we don't have a cat?" She took a seat at the table. "I mean, don't most farms have cats?"

Mrs. Vetter shook her head as she pulled out the pitcher of fresh milk. "I don't know, Ruby. I guess I never thought about it." She sat down at the table and had a snack with her new daughter and they discussed the other friends Ruby was getting to know at the junior high school.

Annette and Terry got home twenty minutes later, and after changing, Annette went right out to the barn to do her chores. After a brownie and some conversation with Ruby and Mrs. Vetter, Terry had his chores to do, and Ruby went upstairs to do her homework.

The phone rang and Mrs. Vetter, who had just started supper, went into the dining room to answer it. "Hello?"

"Hi, Mrs. Vetter. Is Annette home yet?" said a familiar voice.

"Oh, hello, Tim. Well, she's out in the barn right now."

"I should have known."

"Would you like to leave a message?"

"Uh, no thanks, Mrs. Vetter. I'm going to be busy in the barn. I'll catch her later. Bye."

"Bye, Tim." Mrs. Vetter hung up.

Outside with Ginger in the barn, Annette milked the cows and mulled over the situation with the two boys in her life. She still liked Pete Randt. He had looked expectantly at her in Geometry class when Mr. Edwards had announced over the intercom about the Valentines Dance. Was Pete expecting her to ask him to the dance? After all, she had gone to Homecoming with Pete ... *and* his cousin, Luke Elliott.

But then there was Tim. She wanted to ask *him* to the dance. But why would he choose to go with Annette when there were so many other girls in school who also liked Tim? She knew Penny's brother had a reputation for being a lady's man, and she knew he could have any girl he wanted. So why would he want to go to the Valentines Dance ... or any dance, for that matter, with a sophomore?

She sighed as she thought more about it. How was she to compete with junior and senior girls at Ravensville High? At least with Pete, she knew he'd probably accept. After all, they had held hands all the way through the Christmas pageant at school five weeks ago, and all her friends still considered him to be Annette's boyfriend.

"But what about Penny?" Annette mused, and watched as Ginger's eyes focused on her from his resting spot on the hay. "Penny likes Pete now, too. And I think he likes her ... a lot, in fact." She sighed again. It was true that Penny had always liked Steve Newton, a popular sophomore boy. But it seemed that Steve was too stuck up to ask Penny out, so she had pretty much moved on. Penny had been attracted to the Randts' farm hand, Reid Anderson, over Thanksgiving, when the two girls had baby-sat while Pete's mother had baby Laura. But Reid was long gone, and Penny certainly wasn't mooning over the likes of Reid.

"I don't know what to do," Annette said to herself as she finished up and treated the cow's teats with iodine. She did want to go to the Valentines Dance. Neither she nor Penny had the courage to ask anyone last year.

But now they were sophomores …

That evening, when they sat down for their evening meal in the dining room, Terry's and Ruby's uncle, Will Knutson, called. Mrs. Vetter answered the phone.

"Well, hello, Will!" she exclaimed.

Everyone perked up at the mention of Uncle Will's name. Ruby smiled over at Annette, who was chewing on a pork chop.

"Why, that would be just fine," said Mrs. Vetter into the phone. "We'll be expecting you tomorrow evening, then. Oh … and do drive carefully."

"Is Uncle Will coming to visit?" Ruby cried excitedly as Mrs. Vetter replaced the telephone.

"He is." Mrs. Vetter took her place again at the table.

"I'll sleep out in the barn," said Terry, and Mrs. Vetter looked shocked.

Annette and Ruby giggled.

Terry smiled as he reached for his glass of milk. "I'm only kidding."

"Uncle Will *likes* the couch," said Ruby. "He told me so." Then she added, "I guess I'll go to Kay Randt's house next week instead."

"Well, I'm going to bake an apple pie," announced Mrs. Vetter with a gleam in her eye.

Annette wiped her mouth with her napkin and looked at the happy faces at the Vetter dinner table. It felt truly wonderful to have a family.

3

Some Missing Cattle

The next morning in school, Annette avoided the senior
hall. She was sure that her birthday card to Tim had backfired. He was probably embarrassed because of what she had
written inside. A horrible feeling of guilt overshadowed her as
she dragged through her morning classes.

Only in Art class second hour was she able to distract
herself from dwelling on her impulsiveness as she worked on
her clay sculpture and chatted casually with other students
working at her table. The earthy, sweet smell of the clay always
calmed her. It felt good to feel the wet substance in her hands
as her fingers blended and smoothed the piece of clay into
whatever she wanted. If only it was that easy to create what
you wanted in life with another person.

Pete had been on the bus that morning, as usual, and
Penny had chatted freely with him as they rode into town.
Terry had remained quiet for the most part, sitting behind the
girls, and Annette had thrown in her two cents in order to keep
her spirits up. But she was worried that Pete expected her to
ask him to the Valentines Dance, which was exactly two weeks
away.

Oh well, she still had time to make up her mind about

what she was going to do. Maybe she should speak to Penny about it, and see if Penny wanted to ask Pete to the dance. Ever since they had talked about Pete on their walk to the old abandoned tower in December, they avoided the subject. But it was becoming more obvious to Annette with each passing day that Penny was growing fonder of the farm boy Annette had been crazy about just over a month ago.

In the cafeteria during noon hour, Annette and Penny went through the food line, and then Penny said, "There's a couple seats at Lisa's table. Let's go sit with her and Nancy."

Looking up, Annette saw Lisa Kowalski, the FFA president, sitting with their friend, Nancy Marshall. She grabbed an extra napkin and a small carton of milk, then followed Penny through the crowded lunch room. Loud talking and sounds of laughter filled the air as they made their way to the table and sat down.

Annette's eyes skimmed the room and she noticed Tim sitting in the far corner among a group of loud senior boys as they ate their lunch. She immediately diverted her eyes, not wanting him to think she was searching for him. A pang of regret plagued her, which she hoped would soon go away.

"Hi!" Lisa greeted them with a smile. The senior girl picked up her spoon and scooped up some green gelatin that had small bits of peaches and pears in it.

Nancy smiled a greeting at Annette and Penny, then turned back to Lisa. "Tell them about your missing cattle," she said.

"What missing cattle?" Penny leaned forward, so she could hear better, and Annette turned her full attention on Lisa.

"Well, it happened earlier in the week," Lisa explained. She spooned the Jello into her mouth and swallowed. "Dad discovered we're missing four steers."

"What happened?" Penny was alarmed.

"We don't know."

Nancy spoke up. "They think they were stolen."

"What?" cried Penny.

"You mean … rustlers?" asked Annette. "Like, cattle rustlers or something?"

Lisa shrugged. "We don't know."

"Did they break through your fence?" asked Penny.

"Dad and my brothers checked everything already," explained Lisa. "There was no evidence of it."

"No tracks?"

"They looked," said Lisa, "but, of course, you know we've got four hundred acres."

"Gosh," said Penny. She picked up her fork and dove into her mashed potatoes and gravy.

"I thought that kind of thing only happened in the old Wild West," Nancy remarked. She bit into her cookie bar.

Annette smirked and started into her meat loaf.

"Well, I'd better let Tim and my dad know about it," said Penny.

"But your herd usually stays close to the barn this time of year," Annette reminded her.

"Yeah, well, it never hurts to be on the lookout," said Penny.

When Annette got home later that afternoon, Uncle Will's yellow station wagon was parked in the driveway. Her mother's car was gone as Mrs. Vetter had to work that day. Annette knew her mother would be home by suppertime.

Ruby was inside the house with Uncle Will. A man of medium height, he had sand-colored hair that extended in flattened wads here and there on his squarish head. A light mustache, blue eyes and white eyebrows expressed kindness and a gentle soul. He had on loose flannel pants and wore a tan pullover sweater.

They were having an afternoon snack of left-over brownies at the small kitchen table when Annette walked in. Uncle Will smiled at Annette in greeting. Ginger sat near them on the kitchen floor. He stood up and wagged his tail when he saw Annette.

She put her books down and then hung up her coat. "Are there any of those left?"

"We saved one for you … and Terry." Ruby's blue eyes twinkled, and Annette noticed the girl had a smudge of chocolate below her lip.

"Where is Terry?" asked Uncle Will, looking around.

"Oh, he'll be home for supper," said Annette. "He had to go help out at the Duncan farm."

"He works for Mr. Duncan sometimes," piped in Ruby.

"Well, I'm glad he's got a job," said Uncle Will, "even if it's only part-time."

"What have you been up to?" Annette asked him. She opened the refrigerator to take out the pitcher of milk and grabbed one of two remaining brownies on a covered plate.

"Oh, the usual." Uncle Will leaned back in the kitchen chair and rubbed his mustache. "Workin' … and just checkin' up on this young'un here."

Annette joined them at the table, and Ginger settled down at her feet. Ruby stared at her uncle with a fixed smile on her face. Suddenly, she stood up, then walked over to him and threw her arms out to give him a hug. "I love you, Uncle Will."

He laughed as he accepted the hug and patted her back. "There, there, Ruby. I'm just glad you're so happy living here."

Ruby turned to Annette. "Can I show Uncle Will the chickens?"

Chewing a mouthful of brownie, Annette nodded. "Sure," she mumbled, wiping her mouth. "Why don't you feed them, check their water and collect the eggs?"

"Okay!" Ruby pulled Uncle Will to his feet. "Let's go."

"I'll be out to milk the cows in a couple of minutes," said Annette.

Ginger got up and shook himself, ready to accompany the girl and her uncle outside. After Ruby and Uncle Will put their coats on and left the house, Annette gathered up their used drinking glasses, put them in the sink, then went upstairs to change clothes.

As soon as she came back downstairs, she donned her farm coat and went out the door. The telephone rang ... but she didn't hear it.

In a darkened hospital room, Nurse Kim-Ly brought a pan of warm water, a bar of soap and the cleanest towel she could find, to the bedside of the tall man who resembled a bag of bones underneath the dirty blanket. Dusk had settled in and the night sounds of insects surrounded the small grass hut.

In the next room, the doctor was performing a surgical procedure on a dying American serviceman. There wasn't enough anesthesia, so the poor man's wailing rang through the hospital's thin walls. Kim-Ly crouched beside the patient on the cot before her. He was barely conscious, his eyes closed. He had arrived earlier that day, alongside the other man, and he had been barely able to walk. His body had been savagely beaten and was covered in bruises, abrasions, and both arms were broken.

Kim-Ly was only 16 years old, yet she had become a jungle nurse out of a desire to learn more about medicine, as opposed to her older sister, who had run away last year to escape a life of despair. Kim-Ly's parents had begged Doctor Nguyen, whom they had befriended a year ago, to take Kim-Ly and train her to be a nurse. It had taken a lot of convincing on their part, but the doctor could see that she was smart and willing ... and not afraid.

"I must clean your wounds," Kim-Ly spoke softly to her

patient, knowing he could not understand her language, and probably did not even hear her voice. She dipped the towel into the water and wrung it out, then lifted the blanket and began to gently wash away the scum and the blood.

The man groaned, but he did not awaken. He had no dog tags—no identity whatsoever. She pitied him and doubted that he would ever leave this place. Yet she believed in dignity, and she would do her best to clean his body and make him comfortable in whatever time he had left.

Supper was on the table in the Vetters' dining room when Terry came into the house after returning from the Duncans' farm. "Hello, Uncle Will," he called as Ginger trotted over to lick his hand.

"Hello yourself." Uncle Will flashed a quick smile beneath his blond mustache, then passed the bowl of green beans to Mrs. Vetter, who sat to his left. Ruby and Annette were already eating, and Terry washed his hands in the sink, then took his seat on the other side of his uncle. "How do you like working on a dairy farm?" asked Uncle Will.

Terry reached for a slice of bread and picked up his butter knife. "I like it fine," he said.

"Annette's teaching me to milk the cows," said Ruby across the table from her brother. "I had my first lesson tonight."

Uncle Will laughed. "You're gonna have to practice, Ruby."

"I know," she said, "but I did finally hit the bucket."

"Well, you're an expert with the chickens already," said Annette, reaching for her glass of milk.

"How was work today, Mom?" asked Terry.

Mrs. Vetter smiled, and Annette noticed a glow on her mother's face that hadn't been there a month ago. "Oh, it was interesting," she replied, dishing some green beans onto her plate. "Every day is different. And now that I'm only working part-time, there are always new patients to get to know."

"Kay Randt is going to give me a kitten," announced Ruby.

All heads turned and Mrs. Vetter looked up in surprise. Annette stifled a giggle, then asked, "The Randts have kittens?"

"Oh, yes," said Ruby. "Kay says they're real cute. I'm going to pick out the cutest one."

"Mom?" Annette grinned at Mrs. Vetter, who looked a little flabbergasted.

"Well … I don't know about this." She blinked her eyes. "But … well, I really don't see why not." She looked at Will for help. "Do you think it's a good idea, Will?"

Uncle Will settled back in his chair and smiled at her. "What? For Ruby to have a cat? I think it's a splendid idea," he said.

"Why not?" Annette grinned. "Terry, what do you think?"

Her brother was chewing some pot roast, but smiled and nodded.

"That means yes," said Ruby. "Oh, boy, I'm going to have my very own kitten!"

The discussion at the dinner table revolved around cats and dogs. Annette ate her meal silently, secretly wondering if Tim Duncan was going out on a date with someone tonight. It never used to be a concern to her until lately. Since he had just turned 18 the day before, she imagined he probably was going out to celebrate with his friends tonight. She sighed, still bothered that she hadn't heard from him since giving him the card.

After supper, Annette and Ruby washed and dried the dishes while Mrs. Vetter and Uncle Will visited in the living room. Terry was upstairs in his room, and Annette only half listened as Ruby talked about school, her new friends, and the new kitten she was getting soon.

The telephone rang just as they were finishing up, and Annette went to answer it. "Hello."

"Annette!" It was Penny.

"Hi, Pen."

"Guess what? Doc Slater was just here. Remember what Lisa Kowalski said about her dad's cattle coming up missing?"

"Yeah …" Annette was suddenly very interested and draped the dish towel over the back of one of the dining room chairs. Ruby had gone into the living room to be with the adults.

"Well," continued Penny, "Doc Slater told my dad that some other farmers have also been missing some cattle … *and* horses."

"Horses too?"

"Oh, Annette, something's going on. I hope they don't bother anyone else. Who do you think could be doing such a thing?"

"What else did Doc Slater say?" pressed Annette.

"Not much," admitted Penny. "He just wanted Dad to be aware of the situation."

"Geez …" Annette lowered her voice. "By the way, is Tim out celebrating tonight?"

"Oh … you mean for his birthday?" Penny laughed. "As a matter of fact, he did go out for the evening."

Annette's heart sank. "Well, I figured he would," she said. "After all, he just turned 18."

"What are you doing tonight?" asked Penny. "Wanna come over and shoot some pool?"

"I can't," said Annette. "Uncle Will is here. I feel like I should stick around. You know …" What she didn't tell her best friend was that it didn't seem worthwhile to go over to the Duncans' tonight if Tim wasn't home. Instead, she asked,

"Have you talked to Pete?"

There was a brief silence, and then Penny replied, "Me?"

"Yes." Annette giggled. "I just thought …"

Penny let out a big sigh, then said, "Annette … I've noticed that you don't pay attention to Pete as much as you used to. I really didn't want to say anything, but …"

Annette cleared her throat. "Penny, if you want to ask Pete to the Valentines Dance, you should do it."

"What!" Penny was aghast. "You mean, you're not going to ask him?"

Her silence gave her away.

Penny sighed again. "Oh, Annette … I'm so sorry. It's all because of me, isn't it? It's all because Pete has feelings for me. I told you I never ever wanted to come between you and your boyfriend."

"Penny, if you have to know the truth … I can't decide who I want to invite to the dance."

"*Meaning* …?"

"Gad … do I have to spell it out?" Annette caught Ruby's face staring in at her from the living room. She tried to lower her voice more. "Penny … Pete's acting like he wants me to ask him to the dance, but you know as well as I do that Pete's more interested in *you* right now."

"Oh, Annette … *I'm so sorry* …" Penny sounded legitimately agonized over the situation with Pete. There was a long silence, and then Penny said, more cheerfully, "Well, maybe I should ask Steve Newton."

Annette guffawed.

"Yeah, you're right." Penny giggled. "Scratch that." Then she relaxed. "Well, listen, I know you're busy tonight with Uncle Will there, but tomorrow or Sunday, maybe you and Terry … and Ruby, too … can come over and we'll have a pool match."

That sounded good to Annette. She was ready to end the

conversation before she said something she would regret …
about Tim. She and Penny exchanged their goodbyes, and then
she hung up the phone.

"Come on in here, Annette," called Ruby. "Uncle Will
wants to play Scrabble."

Annette joined her family in the living room, but her heart
was aching. At least she had the distraction of a board game to
keep her mind off Tim being out on a date with someone. She
knew she just had to get used to the idea that Penny's brother
was, after all, more than two years older than she was, and
next fall he would be going off to college somewhere.

Maybe she would call Pete and ask him to the dance …
tomorrow … or the next day.

4

Ice Cream Outing

"No! *No!!!* I can't … I *won't!*"

Annette awoke in the dark to Ruby's yelling. The girl next to her in bed was thrashing and gasping for breath. "Ruby … wake up," Annette told her, then reached over to turn on the bedside lamp.

Ruby's eyes fluttered open when the light came on. Annette immediately reached over and put her hand on the girl's arm. "Oh … oh … no …" Ruby immediately burst into tears and buried her face in her hands.

"It's okay, Ruby," soothed Annette. "You were dreaming. That's all."

Ruby continued to cry. "It was awful," she sobbed. "Oh, Annette, I'm sorry to wake you."

A light came on in the hallway. A moment later, there was a knock on their bedroom door, which had been left ajar. "Annette? Ruby, are you all right?" It was Terry's concerned voice.

"She had a nightmare," called out Annette.

Terry pushed the door open and stepped in, dressed in light green flannel pajamas. His medium-length blond hair was in disarray. "Ruby," he said, "calm down … it's going to be all right."

Ruby sniffled as her sobs subsided. She climbed out her side of the bed and ran over to her brother, who gave her a hug. Annette sighed and pulled the blankets up over herself as she sat in bed, watching the two of them.

"It's all right, Ruby," Terry continued to croon. "You're safe. No one is going to hurt you."

"Terry's right," added Annette. She touched her chest and could feel her heart still pounding.

Ruby finally wiped her eyes and looked at the two of them. "These dreams," she said. "I just don't have any control over them. I'm sorry, Annette, and I didn't mean to wake you up either, Terry." She sighed. "I hope I didn't wake Mom." She sat down at the bottom of the bed.

"Do you want to talk about it?" Terry asked. He sat down beside his sister.

"No. I just want to forget about it," said Ruby. There was a long silence as her breathing relaxed. Then she attempted a timid smile and said, "It must have been that apple pie."

Terry chuckled. "Maybe so. I was having a pretty wild dream myself."

"Oh? What was it about?" asked Ruby.

Terry shrugged. "Ah … it's no big deal."

"Oh, come on, Terry," begged Annette.

"Was it good or bad?" Ruby wanted to know.

"A little of both," admitted their brother.

"Well, I'll tell you what *I* was dreaming about," ventured Annette and grabbed her knees over the blankets.

"What?" Ruby stared at Annette curiously.

"Oh, gosh …" she said, "I was in Colorado … at the Mitchell ranch, and we were riding horses in the hills. You and Terry were there, riding along with Penny and Mandy and me."

"That was a *good* dream," said Ruby, "not scary like mine. I wish I had good dreams, Annette."

"Why was it scary?" asked Annette.

Terry shook his head at her, to discourage her from making things worse.

"Never mind," Annette said quickly.

"My dreams are crazy sometimes," admitted Terry. "All I know is, all kinds of weird things were going on. I guess that's pretty normal … right?"

Annette nodded, then made room as Ruby crawled back under the covers beside her. Terry stood up and rubbed his mussed-up hair. "Are you going to be okay?" he asked his little sister.

Ruby was already curling up on her pillow. "Yes," she murmured and her eyes closed.

"Thanks, Terry," Annette called as he walked back out into the hall. A moment later, the hall light went out and then Annette reached over and turned off her bedside lamp.

Ruby's nightmares were disruptive and disturbing to everyone, and most of all to Ruby. Annette wondered if she should talk to her mother about having Ruby see a professional. After all, her traumatic experience at the foster home after the sudden death of her mother was probably plaguing the 13-year-old, who was ordinarily happy-go-lucky.

She listened for a few minutes until Ruby's breathing indicated that she was fast asleep. Then Annette snuggled down into the warm blankets, closed her eyes, and soon drifted off as well.

Annette's mother had the day off from work on Saturday. She planned on driving into Ravensville to do some grocery shopping that morning. Uncle Will planned to stay an extra night, which delighted them all. Terry had been called over to the Duncans' to work for a few hours.

After lunch, Uncle Will asked Annette and Ruby if they wanted to ride into town with him. He wanted to take them to

Woolworths' drugstore for ice cream.

"Sure!" agreed Ruby.

"That sounds fun," added Annette.

"Well, let's go then."

Leaving Ginger behind, the girls climbed into the back seat of Uncle Will's yellow station wagon and laughed at Uncle Will's jokes as he drove the six miles into Ravensville's downtown. No one had brought up Ruby's nightmare and she acted as carefree as ever in the daylight.

"Uncle Will, why aren't you married?" Ruby asked as he drove.

Annette gasped, then stifled a giggle.

"What kind of a question is that?" Uncle Will was obviously taken by surprise.

"I was just wondering," said the girl.

"Well, Ruby," said her uncle, not at all disturbed by her question, "I never really had the opportunity to have a wife."

"Why not?" asked the girl. She leaned forward and held onto the back of his seat. "Don't you think it would be nice to marry somebody?"

Annette exchanged glances with Ruby, who suddenly burst into giggles.

"I think you're trying to corner me," said Uncle Will and turned to wink at Annette.

"Answer the question, Uncle Will."

Will cleared his throat, then took a deep breath. "Ruby, marriage isn't for everyone."

"You mean, you like being alone?"

"Yes." Will nodded his head. "Actually, I do. I really haven't given it a thought, but yes … I like being by myself. I like it a lot, in fact."

Annette remembered that Ruby had told her that Uncle Will was a loner. She was relieved that Ruby didn't pursue the line of questioning. Soon they arrived downtown and Uncle

Will parked across the street from the drugstore.

"Well, young ladies, here we are," he said, turning off the car engine.

It was a gray day on this first day of February. Annette noticed the snow-laden streets were brown from cars driving on them and the snow plows coming through with sand. The naked trees still wore coatings of crusty snow, and the air felt icy and dry as they climbed out of the station wagon and stepped onto the sidewalk in front of a line of stores on Ravensville's main street.

There were only a few people in the drugstore, mostly shopping. Annette followed Uncle Will and Ruby to the counter in back, where a couple of people sat, talking. They took seats on adjacent stools and the waitress, an older lady with glasses and short brown hair, dressed in a red and white outfit with a little red hat, smiled at them and stood, holding her little notepad and a pencil.

"What can I get you?" she asked.

"Well, let's see now," said Uncle Will, turning to the girls. "Ruby?"

"I want a banana split," she said right away, and the waitress wrote down her order.

"Annette?" Uncle Will turned to her with a smile.

"Oh … well, I think I'll have a … hot fudge sundae," she said.

"Good choice," said Uncle Will. After studying the menu before him, he looked up at the woman and said, "Just coffee … with cream and sugar."

"That's all you want?" asked Ruby as the waitress walked away with the order.

An older, heavyset man, dressed in overalls and a sheep-skin coat, sat down at a stool at the other end of the counter. Uncle Will noticed him and said out loud, "Well, I'll be … if it isn't Fred Pruett."

"Who?" asked Ruby.

"Fred?" called out Uncle Will.

Immediately, the man in overalls turned to look at them. He squinted, then tilted his head. Annette noticed bushy gray eyebrows and a thick, bristly gray mustache on a weather-beaten face with wrinkles. "Will?" he called out. "Will Knutson?"

"You old cuss," called out Uncle Will.

The older man stood up and approached them. With a big smile, he reached out his hand and Will shook it in friendship as both men chuckled. Both Annette and Ruby stared.

"Who're *these* lovely young ladies?" asked the man.

Uncle Will spun around in his stool. "This is my niece, Ruby, and this is her new sister, Annette Vetter."

Fred Pruett extended his hand and Annette shook it, then Ruby took a turn. "Must be Ruth's girl," he muttered.

"That's right," said Uncle Will. He turned to the girls. "Fred here worked with me years ago for the Department of Natural Resources." He turned back to his friend. "By the way, when did you retire?"

"Five years ago," said Fred. "Me and the wife bought a farm outside Ravensville and we're raising horses."

"Really?" Uncle Will nodded his head, studying his friend.

"You still working for the DNR?" Fred asked Uncle Will.

"Ya … outta Madison. I'm up for the weekend, visiting the kids." When Fred looked puzzled at that response, Uncle Will tried to explain. "You see, the kids came to me a little over a month ago … Terry and Ruby … as for their mother … well, I won't get into that now. It's a long story."

"Well, what a coincidence meeting you here." Fred grinned. He looked at Annette and stroked his chin. "You're Ruby's new sister?" he asked.

"Annette's mother is adopting me," Ruby spoke up

proudly. "That makes Annette my sister."

"Oh, I see." Fred nodded, then rolled his eyes toward Will and shrugged.

"Horses, eh?" asked Will. He invited Fred Pruett to sit down next to them, which he did, and the waitress came and took his order for coffee and a slice of blueberry pie.

"What other kind of pie ya got?" Uncle Will asked before the waitress walked away with Fred's order.

The waitress quickly went through the different varieties of pie, and Uncle Will said, "Bring me a piece of that blueberry. I'll try it." Then, he and Fred Pruett fell into a conversation about friends they had known and worked with for the State Parks.

Annette and Ruby sat and listened, and looked around at the store and the shoppers in the aisles. The waitress soon brought their desserts and they quietly ate their ice cream. Uncle Will and his friend drank their coffee and laughed about the good old days.

"Aren't you planning to get a horse, Annette?" Ruby asked as she stabbed a piece of banana with her fork, then popped it into her mouth.

"Penny and I have been saving for one since last year," replied Annette.

"How much do you have saved? When are you gonna buy your horse?" asked Ruby, interested.

"Well …" Annette had almost finished her sundae. "We have about forty dollars in our bank account. It might be a long time before we can get a horse." She sighed.

"Kay wants to get a horse someday, too," said Ruby.

Annette grinned. "I know, Pete told me Kay likes horses. I'm glad Kay is your friend."

Ruby smiled and went back to her banana split.

The horse conversation must have reached older ears, because suddenly Uncle Will turned to his friend and said,

"You know, I wouldn't mind driving out to your place to see your spread. These girls here, I'm sure, would like to see your horse operation."

Fred lifted his coffee cup and nodded. "Well, why not *now?*"

"How about it, Annette?" asked Uncle Will.

Annette looked up in surprise. "Horse operation?"

"Fred's horse farm," said Uncle Will. He turned to the older man. "Annette and a friend of hers plan on buying a horse from what I hear. Maybe you're the man they want to talk to."

Fred Pruett laughed. "I have a pregnant mare right now," he said.

"You do?" Annette's blue eyes widened.

"Yep, she's due to foal in the spring. You're welcome to drive out and check it out. In fact, this afternoon's a good time. Will, why don't you follow me out when we get done here?"

The two men continued to talk, laugh and reminisce. Ruby looked up at Annette and smiled. "Maybe your horse is closer than you thought."

Annette sighed. She knew they were a long ways from being able to afford the horse of their dreams, but it was exciting to think that she finally knew someone who raised horses and might be able to sell them a colt or a filly … when they had enough money, that is.

It was morning when Kim-Ly awoke and visited the hospital hut in the jungle outside her village. She didn't expect a pleasant outcome. Her patient was too far gone, yet she had done her very best to clean his filthy, abused body and administer the care she had been trained to give, even with limited supplies. So, she was startled to find the tall, thin man lying on the cot awake, on his back, staring at her as she tiptoed in.

Even though he looked at her calmly, she approached him

with caution. She had learned from experience that escaped prisoners from the militia camps often were deranged and out of their minds. Most of them had been tortured and driven to madness. Dr. Nyugen had warned her not to become friendly in any way with an unpredictable patient in their care.

The American did not speak. He simply stared at her, without emotion. Kim-Ly finally eased her way to the side of his bed and gently laid a hand over his forehead. His fever was gone. A good sign. He didn't flinch from her touch, but continued to look at her face, which seemed to be questioning why he was there.

"You are a miracle man," Kim-Ly said in her language, knowing he had no comprehension. She reached for the container of drinking water, which had been boiled, then treated with chemicals, and offered it to the sick man. Because of the arm splints, he couldn't lift himself, and since he didn't thrash or yell at her, Kim-Ly bravely knelt at his side and helped him up just enough to sip some of the water from a straw that was in the glass.

He choked a little, then moaned, but eventually was able to swallow some of the water. Then, exhausted and breathing heavily, he leaned back against his bed. His eyes stared up at her and she saw gratitude. For the first time, Kim-Ly allowed herself to smile and said to him, "You are going to make it, Miracle Man."

Penny climbed down the stairs on her way to the living room. She was headed for the upright piano, hoping to get some practice in this weekend. She walked in just as her brother Tim was putting the telephone down. There was a frown on his face.

"Anything wrong?" asked Penny.

Tim rubbed his chin. He had just come in from the barn and was still in his coveralls, though he had removed his boots at the entrance. "I've been trying to call Annette," he said.

"Oh?" Penny sat down at the piano bench and opened one of her music books. "Isn't she home?"

"No," said Tim. "Nobody's there. I tried earlier, too."

Curious, Penny asked, "Why? Are you going to ask her out on a date?"

Tim gave her a sarcastic look. "*No!*" Then he softened. "If you must know, I just wanted to thank her for remembering my birthday."

"Oh, that's right!" Penny exclaimed. "I remember … the card fell out of her purse while we were on the bus. Annette turned so red." Then she lowered her voice. "So … what did she write in the card?"

Now Tim got angry. "It's none of your bee's wax," and he marched toward the stairs and ran up to his room.

Penny turned to the "Adagio" from the *Moonlight Sonata* in her book and prepared to practice it. Then she stopped and thought, *I wonder what's going on with those two …*

5

The Pruett Farm

After they left the drugstore, Annette and Ruby climbed back into the station wagon and watched Mr. Pruett start up his pickup truck parked ahead of them. Uncle Will started the engine and soon they were following the truck as it drove out of town.

Fred Pruett's farm was east of town, and as they turned up a county road heading north, Annette recognized the Kowalski farm ahead. She remembered the conversation at lunch the day before, when Lisa had told them about the four missing steers. The Pruett farm was a mile farther up the road, in an open area that was flatter and had a few scattered trees.

The farmhouse came into view, along with the outbuildings at the end of a long driveway lined with evergreen trees. Annette could see some horses standing outside the barn in a large fenced corral. A small border collie ran to greet them as they pulled up in front of the Pruetts' porch.

"You've done well for yourself, Fred," said Uncle Will after the three of them had gotten out of the car and they stood in front of the house with the farmer. A rooster crowed in the distance. Annette and Ruby bent down to pet the dog as she sniffed the two girls, her tail twitching rapidly.

"That's Tootsie," said Fred in reference to his dog. "She's over friendly. Now, Tootsie … leave those girls alone. They came here to look at *horses*."

Annette and Ruby followed the two men as Mr. Pruett led the way to the barn, where he kept his horses. There was old rusty farm equipment scattered around the place, Annette noticed. Their house was old, and she could tell they were in the middle of fixing things up. She noted the large old chicken coop behind the house as they made their way to the barn.

Inside, their eyes had to grow accustomed to the darker lighting after being outside in the snow. Annette made out an aisle that cut through the middle of the big room, with several stalls on both sides. As they walked down the aisle, she noticed several horse heads leaning out to look at them as they passed.

"The mare's at the end," Fred explained. "She's the one that's gonna foal in the spring."

A horse whinnied on the other side, and another one answered it from the front of the barn. "No, it's not feeding time yet," Mr. Pruett called out to his animals.

Uncle Will started asking his friend questions about the horse business. They learned that the Pruetts were just getting started with breeding and raising horses.

"You must know Doc Slater then," said Annette.

"Oh, sure, of course," said Mr. Pruett. "Dick's been out here a number of times. Good man."

Uncle Will looked questioningly at Annette, and she told him, "He's the local vet."

They came to the last stall, and there stood a beautiful bay quarter horse. She stood about fourteen hands, Annette guessed, and her flanks were just beginning to bulge a little.

"Why does she look so sad?" asked Ruby after Mr. Pruett opened the door to the mare's stall and they walked in. He reached a reassuring hand up to calm the horse, who stirred because of the strangers.

"She's just tired," replied Annette.

"Can I pet her?" asked Ruby.

"Go ahead," said Mr. Pruett as Ruby slowly took a step toward the dark mare and placed a small hand against her neck. The horse's muscles shuddered slightly and she blew air forcefully out her snout. Ruby quickly withdrew her hand.

"It's okay," said Mr. Pruett. "Just pet her nice … she's just getting used to you."

"She's beautiful," said Annette. "What's her name?"

"We call her Sundown," he said.

"I like her." Ruby smiled, still petting the horse, who had now relaxed a bit.

Annette reached up and placed her hand gently on the mare's back. "Sundown … that's a pretty name."

"What are you gonna ask for the colt?" asked Uncle Will.

Fred Pruett chuckled. "Gosh, that depends. I can't quote a price yet, Will. She has to deliver first, and then we'll see what she throws."

"Well, give this girl some idea what it might cost," said Uncle Will. "Annette, how much were you and Penny planning to spend on your horse?"

Annette blushed as Mr. Pruett looked at her curiously. "Uh … I have no idea," she admitted. "Actually, I'm afraid we don't …"

"Fred! Oh, Fred, there you are!" A woman came storming into the barn, and they all turned to look in her direction. A large woman with thick, horn-rimmed glasses and gray braids, wearing a heavy coat, hurried toward them, her face in agony.

"Lucy, for heaven's sake, what's wrong?" called out Mr. Pruett.

"I'm glad you're home." Mrs. Pruett approached them and was shaking. Tears suddenly started streaming down her face as her voice broke. "Oh, Fred … something awful's happened."

"What? Are you okay?" He stepped over toward her.

"I just came back from checking the chicken house for eggs," Mrs. Pruett explained. "There was an awful ruckus in the chicken yard, so I went outside and the rooster and the hens were all stirred up."

"What? Coyotes again?" asked her husband.

"I don't know about that," she said, still shaking. "Fred … you need to see for yourself."

"Well, okay," he said, and turned to his guests. "Will, this is my wife, Lucy. Lucy, you remember Will Knutson?"

Lucy's lip trembled as she forced a smile. "Oh … Will … of course, I remember you. How are you? Please … forgive me … there's something I need to show my husband."

"Of course." Will looked disturbed as he put his hands on Annette's and Ruby's shoulders. "Would you like us to leave? Or should we wait here?"

Fred followed Lucy toward the barn entrance, but turned and told them, "No, you can wait here. I'll be back in a moment." He shrugged, then followed his frantic wife out of the barn.

"Gosh," said Annette, "I wonder what happened …"

Uncle Will sighed and stuck his hands in his pockets. Ruby turned back to the horse and began crooning to the mare.

"Maybe we should go find out," suggested Annette.

"No, we'll stay here," said Ruby's uncle.

It wasn't five minutes later when Fred Pruett returned to the barn. He was shaking his head as he met them with an apologetic smile. "Lucy overreacts sometimes," he said. "For instance, we had a couple raccoons break into the hen house last fall. They destroyed several of her chickens. I had to shoot them, of course."

Ruby cringed and stared at Annette, who turned back to Mr. Pruett, who had pulled out a handkerchief and was mopping his forehead.

"Was a predator bothering the chickens?" asked Uncle Will.

"I'm not sure," said Fred. "But Lucy's sure she heard some kind of ruckus."

"We've had foxes and coyotes come around," Annette spoke up. "It's just part of having chickens."

"Annette here is a veteran chicken farmer herself," said Uncle Will with a proud smile.

"Anyway … I'm sorry for the disturbance," said Fred.

"You need to go comfort your wife," said Will. "Come on, girls, let's head home. Thanks for the look at your stable. We'll talk later."

After goodbyes were said, Uncle Will and the girls left. When they reached the end of the Pruetts' long driveway, Annette looked back and saw Fred coming out of the barn with one of his horses, all saddled up. Apparently, he was going to check out the situation that his wife was so worried about.

"Thanks for the ice cream, Uncle Will," said Ruby as they headed back home.

"It was my pleasure," he said with a gentle smile. "I just better not have spoiled your appetite for the delicious meal your mother is fixing us tonight."

Annette couldn't wait to call Penny after they got home, so she could tell her friend about Sundown and the prospect of buying the offspring, if Mr. Pruett was willing to strike a bargain. Even if that didn't happen, it was still something exciting to dream about in the dead of winter, with spring still six weeks ahead.

Doctor Nguyen examined Kim-Ly's special patient and congratulated her on her attentiveness and compassion for the injured and ailing man. "You have done well," he said with a smile.

"Thank you, doctor." She bowed her head humbly, then

looked up at him and asked, "Will he walk again?"

"Too early to tell," the man said as he packed away his instruments. "At least he is more fortunate than his companion."

Kim-Ly hung her head. She knew the American Doctor Nguyen had operated on the other day had passed away during the procedure. He had tried his best to save the man, but he was just too far gone and had lost too much blood.

As she attended to her patient after the doctor left the room, she wondered what would happen next. She also wondered what this man's name was. Since he had arrived without his dog tags, he had no identity. She was quite sure, however, that he had been in the prison camp of the Viet Cong for many days … perhaps weeks. Yet he had survived, and he had somehow escaped.

Her patient fell asleep as soon as the doctor left the room. Doctor Nguyen had given him a sedative to help him sleep. Kim-Ly tucked in his sheet and gently pushed a few strands of his light brown hair away from his eyes, then stood over him for a long moment, closed her eyes and asked for healing, and then she quietly left the room to tend to the other patients in her care.

"Annette, do you know what tomorrow is?" Penny sounded excited on the other end of the line.

"No … what?" asked Annette, who had just picked up the phone when it rang. She had been setting the table for supper as her mother tossed a large lettuce salad on the kitchen counter in the next room. In the living room, Ruby and Terry were watching television with Uncle Will.

"It's Ground Hog Day!" yelled her friend.

Annette giggled. "So?"

"February second," said Penny. "It's the halfway mark for winter. It means we're almost into spring."

"You're right," said Annette. "And what happens again if

the Ground Hog sees his shadow?"

"If he wakes up and sees his shadow tomorrow morning," said Penny, "then there will be six more weeks of winter."

"And if he doesn't?"

Penny cleared her throat. "If he doesn't see his shadow, then spring is right around the corner."

"Yeah, right." Annette then told her friend about earlier that afternoon, and the trip out to the Pruett farm to look at the horses.

"Oh, I wish I could have come," exclaimed Penny.

"And that Sundown ... what a beautiful mare she is," said Annette.

"Oh, I hope we can get our horse from him," said Penny. "Are any others expecting colts?"

"Not that I know of," said Annette. "I forgot to ask, actually." She then explained how Lucy Pruett had come running into the barn, upset about her chickens, and how Fred had left to check it out.

"How odd," said Penny.

"I know," agreed Annette. "Oh, Mom's signaling me. I have to finish setting the table."

"Are you guys coming over tomorrow?" asked Penny. "You know... to hang out and play pool?"

"Wouldn't miss it," said Annette. She almost asked, *Will Tim be there?*" but stopped herself in time.

"Annette, call everybody to the table. Food's ready!" shouted Mrs. Vetter.

"I've gotta go." Annette hung up and hurried up with her task.

6

The Ground Hog Sees
His Shadow

The next day, Uncle Will gathered up his few belongings and thanked Mrs. Vetter for letting him be their guest. Then, he shook hands with Terry, then Annette … and finally gave Ruby a hug.

"See you in a few weeks," the man said as he winked and left the house.

"Bye, Uncle Will," called Ruby. After the yellow station wagon had gone down the road, she turned to Mrs. Vetter and said, "Kay wants me to come over this afternoon. Do you think I can?"

Annette's mother washed her hands in the kitchen sink. "That sounds fine, Ruby. Maybe your brother would like to drive you over to the Randts'?" She looked questioningly over at Terry, who was sitting at the kitchen table, thumbing through his history book.

He looked up at them and flickered a smile. "Sure. I'll take you, Ruby."

"Annette, do you have anything planned for this afternoon?" asked Mrs. Vetter.

"Penny wants me and Terry to come over for a while."

Annette hoped her mother wasn't about to present her with a long list of chores. She decided to score some points. "How about if I do a load of wash before we go?"

"I was just going to suggest that." Mrs. Vetter smiled, grabbing for the hand towel. "Are you caught up on your homework?"

"No, but I can do that tonight," said Annette, heading immediately for the basement stairs.

"Don't forget to wash the sheets and towels," Mrs. Vetter called.

While Annette was in the basement, putting in the first load of wash, Terry drove his sister over to the Randts' farm. Twenty minutes later, she was back upstairs when he walked in the door.

The two of them dressed warmly and walked to the Duncan farm just down the road. Terry asked if Ruby had experienced any more nightmares, and she told him no. "It doesn't happen every night," she said.

"I'm glad she's making friends," said Terry. Ginger trotted along at his side and the sun was streaming in between the trees, making the packed snow along the road glisten.

"Me too," said Annette. "Kay Randt is a really nice girl. All the Randt kids are super."

When they arrived at the Duncans', Penny greeted them on the front porch. The Cheeze, her half-grown Bratislavian sheep dog, leaped on them, his pink tongue panting in excitement, so that Penny had to scold him. Then, he and Ginger made their greetings and ran off to play in the yard.

Audrey Duncan was sitting in the living room, working on a large jigsaw puzzle spread out on the Duncans' coffee table. Six-year-old Karen, in pigtails, was sticking a piece into the picture and grinned up at them. "I did one," she exclaimed.

"Come on," said Penny, and led Annette and Terry down to the basement, where they had the recreation room and the pool table and stereo.

"Where's Tim?" asked Terry as he pulled off his coat.

"Oh, he'll be back soon," said Penny. "He drove into town for something. Who knows what?" She opened the miniature refrigerator that was in the rec room and turned to them. "What kind of soda do you want?"

Annette walked over to see what they had.

"You got any Fresca?" asked Terry.

"All out," said Penny. "How about an RC?"

"Oh, I see a Dr. Pepper in there," exclaimed Annette.

"Hey, guess what?" Penny's green eyes lit up as she handed the two of them their choices of soda in bottles. "The ground hog saw his shadow this morning."

"Oh, that's right," said Annette, looking around for the bottle opener. "Today is Ground Hog's Day."

"He did … he saw his shadow."

"So that means," said Annette, pondering a moment, "we're going to have an early spring?"

"No," said Penny. "It means … six more weeks of winter."

"I don't see what difference it makes." Annette pried off her bottle cap and lifted the Dr. Pepper to her lips. The fizzle tickled her nose.

"It's going to be six weeks, whether the ground hog saw his shadow or not," added Terry as Annette handed him the bottle opener.

"Who determines all this anyway?" asked Annette. "I mean, what kind of animal is a ground hog anyway?" She took a swig of her pop and leaned against the side of the pool table.

"Isn't the ground hog a woodchuck?" asked Penny.

"Maybe he's a marmot," said Annette.

Terry shrugged and turned away. He wandered toward the other end of the room.

Annette and Penny began a back-and-forth about ground hogs, woodchucks and other large rodents. Penny had read about a traditional celebration in a small town in Pennsylvania, where Ground Hog Day had become famous. "That ground hog's name is Phil," she concluded. "I can't pronounce the name of the town."

"Do you know that town?" Annette called out to her brother.

Terry turned around, but there was a look of despair on his face. He shook his head and sat down.

The girls chatted a few minutes longer, and then Annette noticed that Terry was still stewing. She walked over and put her hand on his shoulder. "Terry, is anything wrong?"

"Oh ... it's just that today ... February second ... happens to be my stepdad's birthday."

"Really?"

Penny joined them, a look of concern on her face. "Ruby's father, you mean?"

"Yeah," said Terry, staring into his lap. His bottle of RC Cola rested, untouched, on the table next to him.

"It must be hard thinking about him," said Annette.

"Tell us about him," encouraged Penny. "What do you remember?"

Terry sighed, then began to open up. "Bob ... my stepdad ... could be hard sometimes. He was in the military, as you know, and he believed in discipline and rules. But he was kind and he could be gentle at times. I grew up as if he were my real father. It was only in the last couple of years that my mom explained that he wasn't my real dad."

Annette sympathized with her brother. "But you didn't know *my* father was your dad until recently," she confirmed.

"Not until my mom's passing," said Terry. "That's when I saw my birth certificate for the first time. She'd never tell me who my real dad was. I guess I'll never understand why she had to keep that secret."

Penny shrugged and took a drink of her soda.

"But Uncle Will must have known," said Annette. "Didn't he?"

"He may have guessed it," said Terry. "He hasn't told me for sure."

"Well, I'm truly sorry about your stepdad," said Penny. "It has to be so hard on you and Ruby, not knowing if he's …" She stopped short of saying the words.

"I'm sure Bob is … *dead*," said Terry and the word caught in his throat. He swallowed it down. "The authorities told us his chance of survival was practically zero. I'm sure he must have perished after his plane went down in those jungles in Vietnam."

Annette felt sorry for her brother. It was bad enough, all he and Ruby had been through, with losing their mother to suicide after she learned about her husband's status of being Missing in Action. She wanted to comfort him, but she didn't know what to say or do.

Suddenly, Terry perked up and took a swig from his RC. "Well, let's get a game going. Who's going to play me first?" He put on a smile as he stood up.

Penny played Terry first, and lost. Then, while Annette was in the middle of a game with her brother, she heard footsteps and looked up to see Tim coming down the basement stairs. Her heart skipped a beat. Their eyes met and she quickly looked away. Then she jerked her cue and missed her shot.

"Hi, Terry. Hi, Annette," Tim called out.

"Tough luck," Terry told Annette, then bent over to set up his shot.

Annette flashed a quick smile in Tim's direction, but felt embarrassed. He was watching her closely and she could imagine what was going through his mind. She remembered the words she had carefully written inside his birthday card, and she wished she had held back from revealing such deep feelings. She was positive she had made a fool out of herself by doing so.

"Where were you?" asked Penny, pushing a lock of dark hair out of her eyes.

"I was just messing around," said Tim as he opened the mini fridge to pull out an RC.

"Hey, Annette, is Terry beating you?" cried Penny.

"Yes," she mumbled.

"It's a first," declared Terry as he took another shot, sending a ball into a side pocket.

They continued to play out the match, and Annette was aware of Penny's brother sitting on his stool, drinking his RC Cola and watching her every move. It made her even more nervous, until she lost the game to Terry.

"Okay, Tim ... your turn!" shouted Penny, picking up a cue and offering it to him.

"No, you go ahead," said Tim. "I'm resting."

"Come on, Penny. I'll rack 'em up," said Terry.

Annette sat down and didn't say a word, all the while feeling Tim's eyes on her. Every so often she would lift up her Dr. Pepper bottle and take a little sip, but she was afraid he would see that her fingers were shaking. Penny and Terry teased each other as they took turns, shooting pool.

Finally, after Terry won another game, they took a break. Penny ran upstairs to bring down a snack, and Terry went up to help her. That left Annette and Tim alone, silently waiting for the other to speak first. Annette wasn't sure how much longer she could bear the silence.

"Hey, how come you didn't call me?" asked Tim in a soft voice.

Startled, Annette turned and looked at him. "What do you mean?"

"I tried calling you at least three times in the last coupl'a days," said Tim. "I left a message with your mom ... and Ruby ..."

Annette shook her head. "Nobody said you called."

Tim sighed. "Gad …"

Annette swallowed, then asked, "What … what did you want to call me for?"

Tim kept a straight face. "I wanted to discuss the birthday card," he said, and took a swallow of RC.

Annette blushed and turned away. "Oh," she said. "That."

Tim stood up and walked closer to her. "Annette … what you wrote …"

"Oh, Tim, I'm so sorry!" Annette blurted out. She felt like she was going to cry. "I … I didn't mean to … I didn't mean to write all that. I feel like a fool."

"What?" Tim looked flabbergasted and backed up. "You didn't *mean* what you wrote? Really?"

Annette studied him. He wasn't teasing her. He was serious. "I … I …"

"Well, I thought it was very nice of you," said Tim. "Thank you, Annette. What you wrote was … lovely." Then he hung his head and said, "But I guess you didn't mean it… not really."

She was suddenly mad at herself because a couple of tears sprang from her eyes, and she tried to rub them away. "I'm so … embarrassed," she said. "I thought … I thought you were disgusted with me."

Upstairs, they heard the phone ring. Tim stared at her, and she didn't know for sure, but now it seemed as if he had believed her when she'd said she hadn't meant to write what she had. Why had she said that? She wanted to explain …

But just then, Penny called down the basement steps, "Annette! Ruby's on the phone."

Wiping her eyes, Annette quickly stood and hurried up the stairs, leaving Tim sitting there. She grabbed the receiver, which was lying on the telephone table in the Duncans' living room. Audrey Duncan and Karen were still working on their puzzle. "Hello? Ruby?"

"Annette!" Ruby sounded excited. "I'm bringing home a kitten."

"What!" exclaimed Annette.

"The Randts let me pick out my new kitty," said Ruby. "Do you think Mom will be surprised?"

Annette didn't know what to say. She hadn't expected the Randts' kittens to be ready this soon. "Well, how old is it?" she asked. "Is the kitten still nursing?"

"No," said Ruby. "They're twelve weeks old, Kay said. They've been in the barn all this time, but they said I can bring her home now."

"Well." Annette couldn't help smiling. Perhaps a small pet of her own might help Ruby through the trauma from which she was recovering. "I'm sure it will be all right, Ruby. When do you want Terry to come pick you up?"

"How about in an hour?"

After Annette hung up the phone, she told the others about Ruby's excitement at getting a kitten.

"I hope Ginger will get along with a cat," said Penny.

"I'm not worried about Ginger," said Annette. "He seems to like all animals."

"Cheeze likes to chase our barn cats." Penny giggled. She had a tray of cheese and crackers and a few apple slices that she was getting ready to take down to the basement.

Terry had already gone downstairs with a bag of chips, and he and Tim were playing pool. Annette put on her best party face and tried to forget the conversation she'd had earlier with Penny's brother. Tim didn't seem bothered at all, so she decided it wasn't worth fretting over. She had obviously gotten his attention with the birthday card, but he wasn't upset or anything. If anyone was upset, it was herself.

7

Clyde

"Need help with the milking?" Terry asked Tim when the time came for him and Annette to leave. She wanted to go home to get Elizabeth and Alice taken care of, plus she knew Ruby was eager to be picked up from the Randts', along with her new kitten.

"No, we're okay." Tim followed them up the basement steps. "Dad'll probably want you over on Wednesday, if that's all right."

While they discussed Terry's part-time hours, Penny led Annette into the hallway, where they could talk privately.

"Annette, is everything all right? You seem kind of … down." Penny's green eyes were full of concern.

"Oh, don't worry," said Annette, pulling on her coat. "It'll pass." She managed a smile.

Penny folded her arms. "I know better." She pursed her lips. "Annette, did you and Tim have a fight?"

Annette quickly glanced over her shoulder, to be sure that the boys couldn't overhear. "No, Pen!"

"*Then* what?" asked Penny. "Tim's acting kind of strange, too. What happened between you two?"

"I'm not sure," she finally disclosed. "I think it's something I …" She didn't finish.

"Well…" Penny sighed. "I'm sorry my brother's so … so

unpredictable."

Annette wasn't sure exactly what her friend meant by that statement. Terry stuck his head into the hallway. "You comin'?" he called to Annette.

"I'll see you tomorrow morning," she told Penny.

Before they reached the door, Tim called out, "See ya, Annette."

She jerked around and shot him a quick smile. He seemed nervous to her, which was odd because Tim was always so carefree and liked to tease her. She didn't know how to take him. She was terribly afraid she had upset him.

Annette called Ginger over, and the collie trotted after them. They walked the short distance home, mostly in silence. Terry seemed engrossed in his own thoughts, and Annette had her own to dwell on. She figured Terry was still thinking about his stepdad, how today was his birthday, and that he had most likely perished in Vietnam.

"After you milk the cows, why don't you ride with me over to the Randts' to get Ruby?" Terry asked when they got to the Vetter farmhouse.

Annette agreed. She hurried to the barn and collected her milking gear. She had a lot on her mind to sort out. She couldn't help feeling that she had just ruined her chances of becoming Tim Duncan's steady girlfriend.

A week had passed and Kim-Ly's charge appeared to be growing stronger. Her "miracle man" was slowly, but surely, healing from the devastating wounds he had received in the prison camp. She continued to nurse him and extended special kindness toward him. He had not spoken a word yet, but she would speak to him in Vietnamese and he would respond with smiles and gratitude in his blue eyes.

On a hot afternoon that same week, there was a disturbance outside the hospital. Some members of the militia were questioning Dr. Nyugen about his patients. Kim-Ly overheard. They were searching for Americans who might have wandered into the village, looking for help.

Frightened that they might come in and discover her special patient, Kim-Ly panicked. She felt she needed to hide him from those men. She could tell by their voices that they were ruthless and would kill her "miracle man," if they suspected he was American. Dr. Nyugen argued with the men outside the thin walls of the hut.

Taking measures into her own hands, the young nurse frantically coaxed the tall American off the cot. He also could hear the voices outside and alarm crossed his face as he stood, leaning against Kim-Ly, barely able to stand. Pain seared through him and he winced.

"Please ... we must go," urged Kim-Ly, trying her best to support him and walk him toward the back entrance. Perhaps she could hide him in the jungle until the men left.

"What are you doing?" Quyen, a nurse a few years older than Kim-Ly, stepped into the room.

"Hurry ... we must hide him," insisted Kim-Ly.

With a worried glance over her shoulder, the older girl rushed over and helped Kim-Ly support the injured American. "Where are you going?"

"Out in the jungle," said Kim-Ly. "We must hurry."

The two girls were able to support the American prisoner of war out the back door. He moaned and they "shushed" him, afraid he would draw attention from the outsiders. Finally, they all but carried him far into the jungle and gently laid him down among brush and tall growth.

"You must stay quiet," Kim-Ly told him and put her index finger over her lips. "No noise ... they must not find you."

He seemed to understand their purpose and huddled down, still obviously in much pain. Then the girls left him and ran back to the hospital.

"Quick … the bed," warned Quyen.

Kim-Ly made up the bed quickly, while Quyen gathered up the medicines and instruments that were close by and were telltale signs of an ailing patient.

Three rough men in loose, dirty clothing barged into the room and looked around. Dr. Nyugen was behind them, still insisting they leave, that he was disturbing his patients.

"I told you," said the doctor, "some men came … about a week ago … I operated. The men died."

The man who seemed to be in charge turned on the doctor and struck him. "Where are their bodies?"

Kim-Ly shuddered and Quyen came over and held her. They backed away from the men.

"You only need to look on the hill," the doctor was explaining. "We burned the bodies several days ago. You will find nothing. The men had no dog tags. They had nothing! Now leave my hospital."

When the ruffians finally left, after sweeping the rooms in the hut in search of evidence—and finding none—the doctor and his two nurses sighed in relief and hugged one another.

"Will they come back?" asked Kim-Ly. She was trembling.

"Possibly," said Dr. Nyugen. "Where is the patient?"

Quyen pointed outside the back door.

"He is not well enough to be on his own," said the doctor. "But I fear those men will be back, looking for him … or others."

"What must we do then?" asked Kim-Ly.

"Go and bring him. I do not think they will return this evening. We will make him comfortable, and then I will make arrangements for him in the morning." He patted Kim-Ly's shoulder and gave a smile of encouragement. "You did the right thing."

It was growing dark when Annette rode with Terry in Mrs. Vetter's car over to the Randts' farm on Gaston Road. They parked in front of the front porch to the yellow farmhouse, and the lights inside indicated lots of children romping around.

Both Terry and Annette got out of the car when Pete came out the front door, pulling on his heavy coat.

"Hi, Pete," said Annette.

"Hi, yourself." He grinned. He nodded at Terry. "Come to get your sister?"

"Yup."

"It's milking time. I'm on my way to the barn," said Pete.

"Annette just got done with hers," said Terry.

Pete gazed at Annette. "Well, I'll see you tomorrow on the bus." He gave her a big smile, then started off on the snowy path to the big red barn.

Ruby stepped out the front door, dressed in her red coat, carrying a bundle in her arms. "Hi, Terry! Annette … wait'll you see!" She carefully made her way down the porch steps.

Annette stepped up close to the girl and saw a gray tabby kitten held in Ruby's arms. "Oh, look … it's your kitty."

Terry stepped over and smiled, running a finger down the little animal's back. In response, it looked up at him and "mewed."

"I think she's cold," said Ruby.

"Let's get her in the car then," said Annette, and led the way to the sedan. Ruby climbed into the back seat. She waved out the car window at blond-haired Kay, who stood at the front door with a big smile on her face.

Annette turned around to face Ruby in the back seat. "What are you gonna name her?" she asked as Terry backed the car down the driveway.

"The Randts named her Clyde," said Ruby.

"Clyde?" Annette made a face. "What kind of a name is that?"

"But it's a girl, isn't it?" asked Terry. "Clyde's a boy's name."

"I know, that's kind of silly," agreed Ruby. "Maybe I can come up with something better than that."

"What are you going to use for kitty litter?" asked Annette, suddenly aware that the kitten would probably have to sleep in the girls' bedroom. "Do we need to stop at Browns' Store?"

"No, Uncle Will picked that up for me yesterday," explained Ruby, stroking her kitten. "When he found out I was getting the cat, he bought a plastic tub and some cat sand."

Annette sighed with relief. "Thank goodness for Uncle Will," she muttered.

As they drove down the road, a large truck pulling a horse trailer passed them. Annette wouldn't have paid much attention to the vehicle, except that she happened to notice the back of the trailer was open. One of its doors at the rear was flying open.

"Terry, did you see that?" asked Annette.

"What?"

"That trailer that just passed us … its back door was flapping open. I wonder if they know."

Terry slowed the car and pulled over. "Think we should alert them?"

Annette turned around to see the truck and trailer behind them. "I couldn't tell if there were any animals inside," she said. "Maybe it wouldn't hurt to let them know their door is open."

Terry shifted into reverse and backed the car up, then turned the steering wheel sharply and started back in the direction the truck and trailer were headed.

Ruby was busy with her kitten, but Annette kept her eye on the vehicle now ahead of them. She noticed a couple of cattle inside the back of the trailer. She was afraid one of them might step out, fall off the trailer and get injured.

"Terry, can you signal them?"

He drove a little faster and was directly behind the trailer. He flashed the headlights a couple of times.

"They don't see us," said Annette.

"And they're speeding up," Terry added. "What the heck?"

The truck and trailer suddenly increased its speed again and took off down the road ahead of them, swerving and swaying dangerously.

"Stop, Terry. It's not worth getting in an accident," warned Annette.

"What's wrong?" Ruby seemed alarmed.

Because it was dark and the roads were still a bit icy, they slowed and watched the reckless driver ahead until he disappeared around a curve.

"Okay, we're going home." Terry slowed, then stopped and turned the car around.

"How strange was that?" commented Annette.

"I couldn't see its license plates," said Terry. "Could you?"

"No, the door was swinging too much."

Within ten minutes they were back home, and Ruby couldn't wait to show Mrs. Vetter her kitten. Annette and Terry followed her into the house and smiled as they watched Ruby introducing the little gray cat to the collie for the first time. Ginger touched his gentle nose to the kitten's face and his large red tail swished slowly in greeting.

Ruby laughed out loud, and she called out to Mrs. Vetter, who came through the dining room door, "Ginger loves her! Mom, come over here and meet Clyde!"

Food was simmering on the stove. Annette removed her coat and went to wash her hands, then came back to the kitchen to set the table for supper. Seeing Ruby all wrapped up in a new kitten spread smiles on all of their faces, and for the moment at least, Annette's worries about Tim Duncan dissolved away.

8

Mother-Daughter Chat

It snowed the next morning, but at least it was a light snow with flurries. Annette and Terry met Penny at the end of the Vetters' driveway and they walked to the bus stop. They filled Penny in on Ruby's cat.

"Clyde! What kind of name is that for a female cat?" cried Penny and broke out in laughter.

Pete was on the bus and was excited when they took their seats at the back of the vehicle. "You'll never believe what happened," he told his friends.

"What happened?" demanded Penny, sliding into the seat ahead of Pete, beside Annette.

"Somebody stole two of our livestock," he revealed.

"What?" Terry slid in beside Pete.

"Oh, my gosh." Annette turned to Pete, whose brown eyes were wide.

"How do you know they're stolen?" Penny asked.

Pete explained that some heifers had been out in the fields yesterday afternoon. They usually came in before sundown, due to the cold weather and needing to feed. When his brother Mark came up short in the count, Mr. Randt and Pete had gone out with flashlights to see if they could find the heifers.

"We saw a fence down near the road on the north side of the property," said Pete. "There were lots of tracks in the snow where it happened, and we believe somebody was parked there yesterday."

"And you think they took your cattle?" asked Annette, astounded.

"Well, we don't know any other explanation," said Pete. "My dad can't afford to have even two heifers disappear like that."

Annette and Penny stared at each other, and then Penny turned to Pete. "Lisa Kowalski's dad lost a bunch of cattle last week."

"That's right, they came up missing," added Annette.

"It sounds really suspicious," said Penny.

Annette gasped and looked at Terry, who seemed to have the same idea she did.

"Last night," he told them, "Annette and I were driving Ruby home, and Annette saw a truck and livestock trailer coming down the road as we left your place."

"The reason I noticed it," said Annette, "was that its rear door was swinging open, and I could see at least two cows inside of it."

"Whoa," breathed Pete, sitting back against the seat.

"We actually stopped and turned around to follow it," said Terry. "We wanted to warn them that the back was open."

"But the truck, when it saw we were following it, took off like a banshee," Annette related.

"Rustlers!" cried out Penny. "It sounds like thieves are going around, stealing livestock."

"But why?" asked Terry.

"To sell on the black market?" guessed Pete. "Gee, thanks for telling me. When we get to school, I'm gonna call my dad. I think he needs to know this."

"Maybe I'd better call home myself," said Penny, fidgeting with her books and her purse.

When they got to school, Pete and Penny went to the school office first thing. Annette went to her locker and hung up her coat and gloves, then started figuring out what books and supplies she needed for her morning classes.

Two junior girls were walking down the hall and she overheard their conversation behind her.

"Are you going to ask Terry Vetter to the Valentines Dance?" one asked.

At the mention of her brother's name, Annette glanced up and recognized the tall redhead whose name was Janet. The other girl had long blond hair and plenty of curves, and Annette knew her name was Susan Reed. She was considered one of the more popular junior girls. Susan laughed and said to Janet, "I probably will, especially now that Mary Ann Maxwell has already asked Tim Duncan."

At the mention of Tim's name, Annette almost gasped. Another glance showed the two girls walking toward the junior hallway, laughing as they continued to talk.

Her heart sank. Mary Ann Maxwell? She knew who the girl was, of course. Mary Ann, a senior, was an intellectual and a real beauty with dark hair and olive skin, who always made Honor Roll. Mary Ann had asked Tim to the Valentine's dance?

Well, there went her chance … she should have known. After all, Tim was very popular with the females at Ravensville High. Annette knew that if she had had the nerve to ask him herself, no doubt he would have made up some excuse. There were plenty of nice-looking girls for Tim to date, and *she* was merely a sophomore.

Annette knelt down in her locker to calm herself, then gathered her books and stood up straight. She would just have to accept the fact … Tim was out of her league.

That afternoon when Annette got home from school, it delighted her to see Ruby laughing and playing with her new kitten named Clyde. The girl was occupied on the living room floor, watching the little gray cat chase a long piece of yarn, at the end of which she'd tied a cloth toy mouse.

Terry had gone upstairs to get started with his homework. Annette sat down at the kitchen table with a glass of milk while her mother washed dishes in the sink. "How was school?"

"Don't ask," said Annette. Her mood had been deflated ever since that morning.

"That bad?" Mrs. Vetter turned to face her, then continued with her chore.

"Ruby's sure happy with that kitten," remarked Annette. "I'm glad she has a pet of her own. I think it's going to help her, Mom."

Mrs. Vetter sighed. "You know, I think you're right." She dried her hands, then turned the stove on to heat up the tea kettle, then came over to sit down at the table with Annette. "I've been concerned about Ruby's state of mind. The bad dreams are an indication that she is still suffering from some trauma."

"It's no wonder," said Annette as she recalled the death of Ruth Foley and then Ruby's foster dad molesting her. "If it hadn't been for Terry showing up when he did …"

"Yes, dear, I know." Mrs. Vetter sighed. "Will suggested we contact a doctor, if Ruby's nightmares continue much longer."

"Well, she was fine the last two nights," said Annette. Ruby had slept peacefully through both nights.

They heard Ruby squeal with laughter in the next room, and then she cried out, "Clyde!"

Annette giggled, then drank some of her milk.

"What's on your mind?" asked Mrs. Vetter. "Did something happen at school today?"

"Oh …" Annette sighed. "I'm just a little confused."

"About boys?"

Annette blinked. "How did you know that?"

"Who is it this time?" asked Mrs. Vetter with a smile.

Annette stretched back in her seat. "Oh, Mom … I don't know whether I should ask Pete Randt to the Valentines Dance or not."

"Well, why wouldn't you? I'm sure he'd go with you."

"It's not that," Annette admitted. She stared out the kitchen window at the gray landscape.

"Are you and Pete at odds?" asked her mother.

"Not really," said Annette. "But … well, I'm not sure I told you this, but Pete and Penny like each other now."

"You mean, as in … girlfriend, boyfriend?"

"I guess," said Annette. "Penny denies it. She tells me she would never do or say anything to encourage Pete or take him away from me."

"So the problem is between you and Penny?"

"Oh, no," said Annette, shaking her head and placing her hands on the table. "It's not that at all, Mom. At the Christmas pageant in December, Pete really noticed Penny for the first time, I think. It was so obvious. He really likes her."

"Oh." Mrs. Vetter's brow wrinkled and she didn't know what to say.

"Anyway, Pete likes Penny now … but he seems to still like me. Only …"

"Only what, dear?"

"Only … now I like someone else." There. She had said it.

"Oh, I get it," said Mrs. Vetter. "And would this someone else happen to be Penny's brother?"

Annette nodded her head, then revealed, "Tim kissed me in the barn on Christmas Eve."

Mrs. Vetter did not act surprised. She smiled and reached her hand out, placing it on Annette's wrist. "And so you and Tim have a thing going …"

Annette grimaced. "Kind of ... I'm not too sure."

"Well, you could always ask Tim to the Valentines Dance," suggested her mother.

"No, that's the problem," said Annette. "You see, Mary Ann Maxwell already asked him."

"Ohhh … I see."

"And besides," said Annette, "why would Tim want to go with me?"

"Why *wouldn't* he want to go with you? Annette, it sounds like you've lost confidence in yourself."

"Well, it's not only that, Mom."

"Then what?"

"Pete. I don't want him to be hurt if he's expecting me to ask him to the dance, and then … I don't know what to do."

"How does Penny feel about all this?" asked Mrs. Vetter.

"Penny knows about me and Tim." Annette sipped her milk.

"And?"

"She's okay with it."

"But what about Pete?"

"I don't think Pete knows … yet," admitted Annette.

"Ah, I see." Mrs. Vetter nodded her head. "Well … relationships at your age can be fluid, at best."

Annette wasn't sure what her mother meant. Just then, the tea kettle whistled and Mrs. Vetter stood up to fill a cup with hot water. She got a tea bag out of the cupboard, then came back and sat down.

"Let me explain," said her mother as she dunked the tea bag into her cup. "When I was young, long before I met your dad … there were boys who wanted to court me."

"Oh, Mom, nobody calls it that anymore," Annette chided.

Mrs. Vetter ignored her. "I had several beaus as a matter of fact." She smiled at the memory. "One boy in particular caught my eye. His name was Charles."

"Was this when you were in high school?" asked Annette.

"Yes, I was 17. Charles was 18."

"Tim is 18," murmured Annette.

Her mother talked on, that dreamy look in her eyes. "Charles was dashing and every girl in school had their eye on him. He took me out a couple of times. My parents weren't very happy about it and insisted on a chaperone."

"Gad," said Annette. "That would be horrible …"

"But … to make a long story short," said Mrs. Vetter. "When Charles found out he wasn't going to get from me what he could easily get from some of the other girls … he dropped me. Just like that."

Annette thought she understood her mother's meaning. "Oh, Mom … how did you deal with that?"

"I had very high morals," her mother said. "Your grandparents were very strict, church-going folks, and they had succeeded at drumming into my head at an early age *not* to fool around with young men who wanted to take advantage of me."

"Did you tell Charles you couldn't …" Annette didn't want to say it.

"Of course," her mother replied. "And he got angry. He rejected me right then and there. And I was crushed … broken-hearted … and I cried my eyes out for days."

Annette had never heard her mother discuss her intimate teen-age years before. She asked, "And did you have other boyfriends?"

"Yes, I dated a few after that," said Mrs. Vetter. "Mostly they were not any of the popular crowd. But I didn't really fall in love until I met your father." She looked off into the distance and sighed as she raised the tea cup to her lips.

"And that was when you were in nursing school?" asked Annette.

"That's right. Tom had already graduated and was working for the state park in Black River Falls," explained Mrs. Vetter. "I still had a couple of months left of college."

"And what happened to Charles?" asked Annette.

Mrs. Vetter's face changed to scorn. "Why, I've never given him another thought ... till today," she said. "I imagine he's old, fat and bald by now." She laughed. Then she suddenly stopped and stared into her tea cup. "I really hadn't given men much thought after your father died. I put my entire self into my career, and kept myself busy working at the hospital ... and raising *you*."

Annette questioned whether she should say it or not, but found herself blurting it out anyway, "And then *Earl* came into your life ..."

Mrs. Vetter looked at Annette sadly. "Yes ... but that's over with. It didn't work out. Not everything works out in life, and Earl Warner was not meant to be a part of our family."

"Sometimes I think you blame me," admitted Annette. "About Earl, I mean. After all ..."

"No, Annette! I certainly do not blame you." Mrs. Vetter stared hard into her daughter's eyes. "That's what I'm trying to tell you ... that love is blind. When you think you've found somebody that you think you really care about, and could spend your life with ... you don't always see the whole picture."

"And so you're saying I'm blind when it comes to Tim?"

"You are so young yet," said her mother. "At 15 you don't really know that much about the opposite sex."

"Thanks," Annette muttered with a roll of her eyes. "Now what was that you were saying about confidence?"

Ruby wandered into the kitchen right then. The kitten loped across the floor in front of her. Ginger, who was sleeping underneath the table, perked up to watch the animal.

"Are you getting hungry, Ruby?" asked Mrs. Vetter.

"Yeah, a little," said the girl, then folded her arms and looked from one to the other. "I couldn't help overhearing some of your conversation." She grinned.

Annette felt her face turning red.

"Mom …" Ruby looked right at Mrs. Vetter and asked, "Why don't you marry Uncle Will?"

Mrs. Vetter erupted in laughter and almost spilled her tea. Annette's mouth opened in surprise as she and her little sister looked at one another.

"Well … don't you think it's a good idea?"

"Ruby," cried Annette, "you're so bold!"

Mrs. Vetter got up from the table, still laughing. She wiped at her eyes, which had started to tear up. "Oh, goodness! Ruby, oh Ruby … are you in the business of arranging marriages now?"

"Well, no," said the girl, suddenly apologetic. "I mean …"

"It's all right," said Mrs. Vetter. "I can understand why you would want Uncle Will to be part of our family."

"He *is* part of our family already," insisted Annette.

"Will is a good friend," explained Mrs. Vetter as she took her empty tea cup to the sink. "I respect him a lot, and I enjoy his visits. But …" She burst out into laughter once more, until her sides shook. When she recovered, she tried to be serious. "But, Ruby … I don't want to marry your Uncle Will. That would ruin everything."

"Who's marrying Uncle Will?" called out Terry's voice as he came down the stairs. He walked into the kitchen, looking surprised at what he'd overheard.

The girls both exploded into giggles and Mrs. Vetter just stood there, shaking her head and wiping her eyes.

Before they could explain about their conversation, the telephone rang. Annette ran into the dining room to answer it. "Hello?"

"This is Fred Pruett," the voice said at the other end. "Is this Annette?"

"Yes, it is."

"May I please speak to Will?"

"Uh …" Annette swallowed, still recuperating from the good laugh they'd had. "Uh … Gee, Mr. Pruett, Uncle Will doesn't live here, you know. He was just visiting for the weekend."

"Oh. Oh, I see." Fred Pruett sounded very disappointed.

"I can give you his number," said Annette. "Is there anything we can help you with?"

"Well." The farmer sighed, then said, "I apologize. We've had a bit of trouble here."

Annette could hear Lucy Pruett in the background, crying and carrying on. "What's wrong?" she asked.

"Well, I guess I don't mind telling you," said Fred. "My wife's chickens have been ransacked."

"What!" Annette was surprised. "Chickens? What happened? Do you have varmints?"

"No, no … at least it doesn't appear that way. I'd say somebody came during the night and made off with about a dozen of Lucy's chickens."

"Oh, no," said Annette. She was thinking about the Randts' stolen cattle and Lisa Kowalski's dad having missing stock. Now the Pruetts. "Have you got any horses missing?" she asked.

"Not that I know of," said Fred. "At least … not yet."

Annette quickly explained to Mr. Pruett how there seemed to be some rustlers in the area, gathering up people's livestock. She suggested he give the sheriff a call and report what had happened.

"Okay, I think I will," said Mr. Pruett. "Lucy, calm down!" he called out, then back to the phone he said, "If you don't mind giving me Will's number …"

"Oh, of course." Annette called to her mother. "Do we have Uncle Will's phone number?"

"I know it." Terry stepped into the room and Annette handed him the phone.

After he exchanged words with the caller, Terry hung up. "What's wrong?" he asked.

"Fred Pruett, Uncle Will's friend who raises horses on the east side of Ravensville, says his wife's chickens were robbed."

Ruby shrieked. "The chickens were robbed? You mean, their eggs?"

"No!" Annette almost laughed, but the situation was serious. "Somebody stole the chickens … about a dozen of them, he said."

"Now that's strange," called out Mrs. Vetter, who had started cutting up vegetables at the sink.

"I'd better get outside and milk the cows," said Annette.

"Supper will be ready in half an hour," said Mrs. Vetter.

"Can I come out and help?" Ruby asked.

"Sure, Ruby. Grab your coat and your boots. You want to try milking one of them again?"

The girl was ecstatic. She looked around for her kitten, and they saw poor little Clyde, curled up on top of the bench near the back door, konked out after her long playing session.

"Don't worry, we'll keep an eye on Clyde," Terry told his sister as he reached into the refrigerator for the pitcher of milk. He and Mrs. Vetter smiled as the girls put on their garments and went out to the barn.

9

Memory Lapse

Kim-Ly's parents had been reluctant when she made her request ten days ago. They knew the danger of hiding an American when they faced the horrors of war on a daily basis. Yet her pleading had finally convinced them that unless they offered refuge, Kim-Ly's special patient, whom she called the "miracle man," would die at the hands of the Viet Cong.

He was brought to their modest home just outside their village during the night, in order to avoid being seen by the other villagers. The good doctor had helped his young nurse, at great risk to himself and his modest hospital in the jungle.

It had been a rough week for the tall, middle-aged man, but he was growing stronger each passing day. Kim-Ly brought what little medicines the doctor could spare, and she made it her mission to heal him.

"What will you do with him when he is able to walk?" asked Kim-Ly's mother.

Kim-Ly had not considered the next step. Her goal was his healing, and he hadn't spoken more than a few words since he and his now-dead companion had stumbled onto Dr. Nguyen's hospital. Fortunately, the vicious men who had come in search of American strays, had not returned. But Kim-Ly and her parents stayed alert and wary. It was good, at least, that the brown-haired, blue-eyed man with his shaggy beard growth did not make a whole lot of noise.

Kim-Ly tried numerous times to learn the man's name. He always shook his head. He seemed to understand a few of the phrases of the Vietnamese language, but appeared puzzled at being able to give his identity.

"Perhaps his memory is gone," Dr. Nguyen explained one afternoon. "He may be suffering psychological trauma and has blocked out his past."

"Then we must give him a name," said Kim-Ly. She smiled and said, "I know. I'll call him Joe."

Quyen, who was wrapping bandages nearby for later use, giggled and said, "That's not a very complimentary name, you know … G.I. Joe!"

Kim-Ly didn't care. Her patient now had a name.

"Ruby, don't be afraid to pull harder," Annette instructed as she watched the 13-year-old milking Alice in the barn. Annette was busy filling the pail beneath Elizabeth.

Alice mooed in response and turned her black head to look at Ruby, who was frowning and not making a lot of progress in her work.

"Here, let me show you once again." Annette got up from her stool and moved toward Ruby and the cow. She placed her fingers in the proper positions and easily squirted milk into the pail. Alice's head turned back, facing front.

"Okay, let me try again," said Ruby, eager to get it right. It took a couple more tries, but then Ruby started getting streams of the rich milk coming out. She grinned with satisfaction.

"That's the way," said Annette and went back to Elizabeth.

While they were doing the milking, Ruby hummed a

familiar tune and Annette smiled over at her.

"What's that called?" she asked the girl.

"It's just a song my dad used to sing when I was little," said Ruby and resumed humming.

"That's nice," said Annette, and after a minute she said, "That's a nice way to remember him."

"Oh!" Ruby stopped humming suddenly, but kept on milking as she turned to Annette with a surprised look on her face. "Oh no, I can't believe I forgot."

"What did you forget?" asked Annette.

"It was my dad's birthday yesterday!"

"Yeah, Terry said something about it when we were over at Duncans'," said Annette.

"And it was Ground Hog's Day," said Ruby. "I completely forgot about my dad on his birthday."

"Ruby, you had other things on your mind," Annette reminded her sister, "such as Clyde?"

Ruby sighed. "Right. Still … I feel awful that I didn't even remember …"

"Well, you did now," said Annette. "Hey, why don't you tell me some more about him? Your dad, I mean."

Ruby brightened as she continued to milk Alice. "Let's see …"

"What does he look like?"

"You mean … what *did* he look like?"

"Ruby, we don't know for sure about your father. He's just Missing in Action."

"Terry says he's probably dead," said Ruby. "I mean, that's why our mother did what she did."

Annette could tell the girl was starting to get choked up. "Well, never mind. Just tell me some good things about him. What was he like?"

Ruby sniffed, then concentrated on the milking. "Okay … well, my dad was kind of tall, and he had brown hair."

"What color were his eyes?"

"Blue."

"My dad's were too." Annette smiled. "Go on. What else?"

Ruby continued. "Well, he was in the Air Force, as you already know, and we moved around a lot before he got sent to Vietnam. He was kind of strict. He really liked to keep everyone on schedule and everything had to be in order. I think I had the cleanest room of all my friends." She laughed. "He got along good with everyone, and he laughed a lot, too. I loved his laugh …" Her voice trailed off into sadness.

Suddenly, the barn door opened and Terry stepped in. "Hey, Annette, Penny called. I told her you were out milking, and she said you can call her back."

"Thanks, Terry." Annette smiled over at her brother, who wandered closer to watch Ruby milking Alice.

"Good girl," said Terry. "I think Annette's gonna make a dairy farmer out of you yet."

Ruby grinned, pleased at the compliment. "We were just talking about Dad," she revealed. "I'd forgotten that Ground Hog's Day was his birthday."

Terry scratched his head and looked at Annette. "Well, I think I'll go help Mom a bit. By the way, she said supper's ready in about ten minutes."

"We'll be right in," Annette called back as he left the barn.

"Terry misses him a lot," said Ruby.

"I can tell," she replied.

"I mean, I know he isn't Terry's *real* father. But still, it bothered Terry a lot when he heard about him."

"I'm sure it did," said Annette sympathetically. "But you know, Ruby, you should never give up hope. Maybe one day soon they'll find your father."

"Oh, Annette, I pray for that every night." Ruby smiled and squeezed the last of the milk out of Alice's udder. "Looks like I'm done."

"I am too," said Annette. "Here, I'll show you how to treat her with the iodine."

"Okay. Maybe I can help again."

"I think that can be arranged." Annette laughed.

Supper was on the table when the girls returned to the house. Terry had already prepared Ginger's food and set the dish down on the dog's mat after they came in.

Later, after she'd helped with the dishes, Annette went into the dining room and dialed the Duncans' phone number. Mrs. Vetter had gone upstairs, and Ruby was in the living room with Terry. She could hear the television going. After three rings, a male voice answered. "Hello. Duncans'."

"Uh … *hi*. Is … is Penny around?"

"Well, hello, Annette." It was Tim. "No, actually, Penny's outside with Karen right now."

"In the dark?" asked Annette.

"Well, actually, they're with my dad in the barn."

"Oh," said Annette, wondering if she should ask him to have Penny call her.

"By the way," said Tim. "Have you asked Pete yet to the Valentines Dance?"

Annette's heart began to race. She wasn't sure how to answer him. His voice sounded a little mocking … so she took that to mean that he had accepted Mary Ann Maxwell's invitation. "Well …"

"He's waiting for you to ask him," said Tim. Annette thought his voice sounded a little strained.

"I'm planning to ask him in a day or two," Annette finally said. She felt very uncomfortable having to disclose this to Tim. She wanted to ask if anyone had asked *him*, but she already knew the answer to that.

There was kind of a long silence on the other end, and

then she heard Tim sigh.

"Are you there?" Annette asked.

"Yup." He sighed again. "Well, I'll tell Pen you called."

"Okay," she said. Another long silence, and then she suddenly blurted out, "Wait, Tim ..." Then, a second later, she changed her mind. She couldn't bear it if he said the words and told her he was going to the dance with Mary Ann.

"What?" he asked gently.

"N-never mind. Good night." She immediately hung up, then placed her hand over her heart, which was still fluttering. With a little gasp, Annette ran out of the room and headed up the stairs to her bedroom to have a good cry.

That morning, "Joe" was able to communicate to Kim-Ly to bring him paper and a pencil. He already realized no one in the vicinity would understand what he wrote, but somehow it seemed to help organize the thoughts that were tumbling around in his head. He wrote:

The young nurse is kind. She's been good to me, but I don't know why. I don't understand her language, but she has told me her name — Kim-Ly — and her parents watch me from the doorway. They watch me with suspicion.

What in the world have I done to deserve their scorn? Maybe they are afraid. Scared, like me. I'm scared, but not just because I don't remember very much. I'm scared because I don't know who I am, or where I come from.

What is my name? Kim-Ly calls me "Joe." Joe ... WHO? I know I am someone else. But I don't know who that is. I know I belong somewhere else. Why can't I remember what happened to me before I awoke on that cot in the bare-bones jungle hospital?

The nurses moved me out of there quickly the day I heard the angry voices — men shouting in their native tongue — and I saw how frightened the girls were. They were scared for me. But I don't understand why they risked their lives for me.

Who am I? I do not belong here. Sometimes, while I dream, I see faces … faces of people who seem familiar to me. But I don't remember them at all. Oh, I wish I did. How I wish I could remember.

Tears of frustration welled up in the tall American's eyes. He placed his pencil and pad of paper down, then lay back, staring up at the flimsy ceiling of the dim room. Outside the sun beat hot against the tropical earth. Beads of sweat erupted on his face and bare chest. The air hung heavy with animal dung and the sounds of insects chirping and buzzing in the humid jungle filled his ears, day and night.

Time stood still.

10

Invitation to the Dance

A whole week passed. Annette sat on her bed on Monday evening, up in her room, studying her science. It was all she could do to try and concentrate on the practice questions.

"If heat is added to a liquid, what occurs?" she murmured out loud, and at the sound of her voice, her collie lifted his ears on the floor beside her. She pondered. "Do the molecules expand? Does the motion of the molecules increase? Or does the state of the molecules turn to a solid?"

She sighed and marked down her answer: "Motion of molecules increases."

Just as she was about to tackle the next question, Terry came out of his room and stopped in the doorway to the girls' bedroom. Annette looked up from her homework and smiled at him.

"You're hitting those books pretty hard lately," he said. "Do you need any help with anything?"

"I have a science test tomorrow," said Annette with a groan.

"Oh." He stuck his hands in his pockets and turned toward the hall stairs, then stopped and stepped inside her room. "I've been meaning to ask you … did you ask Pete to the dance yet?"

Surprised, Annette stared at him. "No." She glanced over at the calendar on her wall. Ruby had put an "X" over all the days that had gone by. "Oh, my gosh, is it really February 10th?" she asked her brother.

"Yes," he replied, cocking his head.

Annette sighed and closed her book. "Valentines Day is Friday."

"That's right," said Terry.

"You're going to the dance with Susan Reed?" Annette asked. She knew Terry had been asked.

"Uh, no ..." He brushed his lips with his hand and smiled. "I'm going with Debbie Kelton."

"What!" Annette gasped. "Debbie asked you? You accepted?"

Terry nodded his head, grinning. "Do you object?"

"No, not at all." She laughed. "Debbie ... oh, I'll bet she's tickled! Oh, I'm so glad you're going with *her*. She's one of Penny's and my closest friends, you know."

"Yes, I know," said Terry.

Annette stood up and stretched, and Ginger took that as his cue to get up and shake himself. "Well, I guess I'd better go downstairs and give Pete a call," she said. Then she stopped and said, "Terry ... did Pete say anything? I mean, is he expecting me to ask him?"

Terry shrugged. "I dunno."

"Did Penny say something to you?" Annette put her hands on her hips.

"Well ... she might have mentioned something ... I mean, she thought you would have asked him last week."

"I don't know why Penny doesn't ask Pete herself," said Annette, and followed Terry down the hall to the stairway. "She knows darn well that I *know* she likes Pete. And he likes *her*."

"I can't help you with that one," said Terry with a sideways glance.

Ruby was in the living room, watching a sit-com with Mrs. Vetter. Her laughter rippled into the kitchen as Annette crossed over into the dining room to the telephone. Terry stayed in the kitchen to get something out of the cupboards.

When she dialed the Randts' phone number, the line was busy. Annette started to put the phone down, then picked it up again and pressed the bar to clear the busy tone. Then she waited for the dial tone and quickly telephoned Duncans'.

After two rings, Penny answered. "Hello?"

"Pen …"

"Hi, Annette."

"Penny, I just realized the Valentines Dance is on Friday night. Are you planning on asking Pete?"

There was a short silence and then Penny clicked her tongue. "Annette, I know what you're trying to do. But I've already told you, Pete wants *you* to ask him to the dance … not me."

"Well, did he say that?" asked Annette. "Come on, Pen, I need to know."

Penny sighed. "Oh, Annette … No, he didn't say anything. But everyone can see that Pete's your boyfriend, and none of the other girls have dared to ask him."

"That's ridiculous." Annette tried to laugh, but it wasn't authentic.

"Annette, just what is your problem?" demanded Penny. "Why are you waiting till the last minute?"

"It's not the last minute. It's only Monday." Then she changed the subject. "Terry's going with Debbie," Annette disclosed. A quick glance toward the kitchen told her that Terry had left the room.

"Wow!" Penny was as excited as Annette had been. "Really! That's great!" Then she lowered her voice. "I guess her crush on my brother must be over." She laughed out loud.

"Who's taking Tim?" Annette dared to ask, her heart starting to pound.

"I don't know," said Penny.

Annette was flabbergasted. "*What?* You mean, you really don't know?"

"He hasn't said anything," Penny revealed.

"But ..." Annette swallowed, then continued, "I over-heard Susan Reed and her friend Janet saying that Mary Ann Maxwell had asked Tim to the dance."

"Well, Annette, he hasn't said anything about it to me," said Penny. She hesitated, then said, "Annette ... were you hoping to ask Tim to the dance?"

Now that she had been caught, Annette had to admit it. "Actually ..."

"Oh, Annette," said Penny. "Why didn't you?"

"Penny ... Tim's a senior."

"And what does that have to do with the price of tea in China?" Penny's voice had turned shrill.

"Penny, Tim can have any girl he wants. Why would he want to go to the dance with me?"

"Annette, bite your tongue," chided Penny. "I can't believe you said that."

"Well, it's true," said Annette. "Tim is very popular, and I'm just ... just a ..."

"Never mind that," Penny reprimanded. "What about Pete? What about *his* feelings?"

Annette sat down at the dining room table, upset by the turn of the conversation. "Well, the truth is, Pen ... I was waiting first to see if anyone else asked Tim. And if no one did, then I would have ... you know ..."

Penny laughed. "You are mixed up, girl!"

"Are you going to ask anyone?" Annette dared to ask. "I mean, have you thought about ..."

"Certainly *not* Steve Newton," cried Penny.

"Well, what about Dennis Schaeffer?" asked Annette. "He took you to Homecoming."

"No, Dennis and I aren't compatible," said Penny. "Oh, hold on a minute. Tim just walked in. I'll go ask him …"

Annette screamed into the phone, "Penny! *Don't!* What are you doing?"

It was too late. In the background she could hear Penny talking to Tim, but she couldn't make out anything that was being said.

Ruby's kitten suddenly romped into the dining room, playing with her catnip mouse. Clyde crashed into a table leg and bounced off. Annette would have laughed at the cat's antics, but she was momentarily in a panic about what Tim might say or do. What if he came to the phone right now and talked to her?

Several seconds later, Penny came back on the line. "Sorry, Annette."

"I can't believe you told him!" Annette's temper started to flare. "Penny, how could you?"

The girl on the other end giggled. "Cool down, Annette. It's not what you think."

"Then what?"

"I simply asked him if he was going to the dance with Mary Ann."

"And?" Annette felt her face flush.

"He said no."

"And what else did he say?" asked Annette.

"He asked if it was you on the phone."

Annette almost collapsed. "This is worse than I thought," she said into the phone.

Then Penny told her, "Tim said you need to call Pete and ask him to the dance … *tonight*."

For several moments Annette could not even speak. She

felt like her heart was in her throat. What could be worse than having the boy she adored suggest that she ask *another* boy to the dance?

"Annette … are you still there?"

"Yes, Pen." Annette sniffed. "Okay. I'm going to hang up, and I'm going to call Pete … right now."

"Call me back afterwards," Penny said a little too anxiously.

Annette was puzzled as they hung up. Not only puzzled by Penny's interference with Tim, but the hint of desperation in her voice at the end of their conversation. She knew, without a doubt, that Penny did care for Pete, and that she truly thought she was doing the right thing by encouraging Annette to ask Pete to the dance because she believed Pete wanted Annette to ask him.

"But what if Pete really would rather go to the dance with Penny?" Annette mused as she slowly dialed the Randts' number.

A nother month had passed. At least that's what it felt like to the tall American who had recovered enough to get out of bed by himself and walk a little. He was uncertain how long he had been a guest in Kim-Ly's parents' house.

In the last few days, Joe had managed to finally gain their trust. Kim-Ly's tiny mother smiled at him with squinty eyes and two front teeth missing. Her husband was small as well, very humble, with kind eyes. He noticed that the women did most of the talking, which he did not understand.

He was still too weak to travel, but his bones were mending, his bruises were fading, and although he was not gaining any weight, at least he was eating regularly. They fed him rice, vegetables, roots and some kind of unidentifiable meat. He didn't want to know what animal it was from.

At night he would dream. Often his dreams would cause

him to awaken in terror. There were recurring scenes in which
he was fleeing on foot through the jungle, and he had a
companion—a man who had been his friend. They were
always fleeing from danger and trying to get somewhere safe.
But he didn't remember what that danger was, or how the two
of them had ended up having to survive in the jungle.

In the quiet heat of the afternoons, when Kim-Ly's mother
brought him tea, he would sit and think about those dreams
and try to recall his memories. Kim-Ly was busy at the hospital,
but usually came home for the night to sleep, and she would
always check on him, smile, and call him "Joe." The language
barrier kept him from asking the many questions he had. How
would he ever get his answers?

Then, one morning at dawn, he saw in his dreams the
faces of a light-haired woman and a small blonde girl. The
woman's face was strained and wrinkled with tears in her
hazel eyes. He knew her. He felt he had been intimate with her,
yet it was fleeting in his memory. Then he saw the girl with big
blue eyes sparkling at him, a smile curling her rosebud lips as
she reached her arms out to him and called, "Daddy!"

That's when he had awakened with a start. He knew the
girl too, and his heart ached. Suddenly he missed her and
wanted to immediately go back into his dream so that he could
find out more about them. He was excited because he was
starting to remember something about his past.

When Kim-Ly stopped to give him some breakfast before
she left for the hospital, he sat up in bed and began babbling to
her about the dream and the family he had somewhere. Kim-Ly
was startled at first, but then she smiled and nodded, equally
excited that Joe seemed to be regaining some of his memories.

"We must find someone who can translate for us," Kim-Ly
told Dr. Nguyen later that morning. "Do you know anyone
who speaks American?"

The doctor was treating one of the villagers who had a

boil. "I must be careful who I ask," he replied. "You know that if we start asking for a translator, those men may come back. We can't risk alerting them."

"No," Kim-Ly agreed. "They have no mercy."

The patient, having overheard them, spoke up. He was an elderly man whom they trusted. "I have a cousin who knows some English," he told them. "He lives a day's walk south, but he is due for a visit soon … perhaps this week, or the next. When he arrives, I will bring him."

"But can we trust your cousin?" asked Kim-Ly.

"You can trust Sinh," the patient assured them with a smile.

11

Learner's Permit

Annette waited while the phone rang at the other end of the line. She was determined to take care of this matter with Pete once and for all.

"Well, hello, Annette," said Mrs. Randt, who had answered. "Hold on and I'll get Pete."

In the background Annette could hear the voices of some of the children, which brought back memories of when she and Penny had baby-sat the Randt children at Thanksgiving time. She remembered fondly how she had envied Pete and his siblings for being a large family. Well, now *she* had a family — a brother and a sister — and so far she was delighted.

"Hello." Pete's voice was breathless and Annette knew he had hurried to the phone.

"Hi, Pete."

"Annette! Hey … how are you?"

"I'm fine," said Annette. "Pete, I really meant to ask you long before now … but do you want to go to the Valentines Dance with me on Friday?"

Suddenly he burst out laughing and Annette was startled. Did he think she was joking? Then he calmed down and said, "Sure. I'll go with ya."

"Great," said Annette, though she didn't think Pete sounded that excited about the idea.

"Uh … how are we gonna get there?" he asked, since neither of them were driving yet.

"Oh, I'm sure Terry will take us in Mom's car," Annette said. "Maybe we'll double with him and Debbie Kelton."

"What … what about Penny?" asked Pete. "Did … did she ask anyone?"

Annette sighed. *Ah-ha* … there it was. She cleared her throat, then said, "Gosh, I dunno, Pete. She didn't say."

He seemed to recover suddenly. "Well, that doesn't matter, does it?" He forced a laugh, then cleared his throat. "I guess I'll see you tomorrow on the bus."

"Yes, you will," said Annette, but then a thought occurred to her. "Pete, before you hang up …"

"Yeah?"

"Did you ever find out what happened to those missing cows?"

"No," said Pete. "But Dad and Mark repaired the fence right away, and the sheriff was supposed to come out, but he never did. I guess it's happened to some others in the county."

"Hm," said Annette. She hadn't heard of any more cattle or horse rustling that week. It was devastating that people were having their livestock stolen, but maybe the culprits had left the area. "Okay then. Good night, Pete."

"Good night, Annette." He hung up.

Ruby had come into the room and Annette just now noticed. "Hi, Ruby."

"You're going to the Valentines Dance?" The girl grinned.

"Yes," said Annette. "I'm taking Pete Randt."

"He's really cute," said Ruby. "I can't wait till next year, when I'm in high school."

"Eighth grade was fun," Annette told her. "Enjoy it while you can. Once you're a freshman, the homework starts getting harder." She got a glass out of the cupboard and poured herself a glass of water from the tap. "And speaking of homework ... I've got to finish studying for my science test."

Ruby went back to the living room, and after Annette took a couple swallows of her water, she suddenly remembered Penny—and how she'd promised she'd call her back about Pete. She started for the phone, then stopped. No, she'd wait and tell her in the morning. She didn't want to risk having Tim answer the phone.

On the way to the bus stop the next morning, Penny asked Annette if Pete had said yes.

"Uh-huh," she replied. "I know I should have called you back, but I had to study for the science test."

Penny seemed to accept that excuse. "Hey," she said suddenly, "isn't today the eleventh?"

Terry nodded his head as he walked alongside them on the snowy pavement. "Just three more days till Valentines Day."

"Oh!" Annette gasped, then stopped in her tracks. The other two turned and looked at her.

"It's your half-birthday," said Penny with a grin.

"Her what?" asked Terry.

"It's the eleventh of February," said Annette. "I'm fifteen and a half today."

"That means she can go apply for her driver's permit," Penny explained as they resumed walking.

"Do you wanna go after school?" Annette asked.

"Why not?" Penny sighed. "Unless my mom has something planned. Is your mom working today?"

Annette shook her head. "No, but she's working the evening shift tomorrow."

"Just think, Annette. We're going to be driving!"

"Oh no," said Terry. "Maybe I'd better put a notice in the

Ravensville Herald that says: WARNING! Annette Vetter and Penny Duncan are learning to drive. Clear the streets!"

"Very funny," mumbled Annette, but Penny snickered.

Pete was on the bus and greeted them as usual as they took their normal seats at the back. He and Terry talked while Annette chatted with her best friend.

"How is Ruby's kitten doing?" Penny asked.

"She's really active," said Annette. "Ruby absolutely adores that kitten."

"Has Ruby had any more nightmares?"

"Actually, no," said Annette. "And that's really a good thing. Poor Ruby … all she's been through. I believe the kitten has helped her."

"Pets can be good therapy," said Penny.

"Therapy?"

"Well, yes," said Penny. "I read a magazine article about how nursing homes are starting to consider having pets around because they help the old people feel better."

Annette smiled. "That sounds reasonable. Gee, I feel sorry for kids who can't have animals."

"I know," said Penny. "But there are some people who have allergies, like my cousin Danny in Green Bay."

They rode in silence for a while, and then Annette spoke up. "Pen, I feel awful that you're not going to the dance."

Penny shrugged. "It's okay. I don't know who I'd invite at this late stage."

Annette quickly glanced back at the boys, who were discussing sports behind them. She lowered her voice. "Pen, maybe if you …" She stopped herself and stared into her lap.

"If I what?" Penny shot a look at Pete, then smiled and looked out the window.

"I don't want to discuss it now," said Annette.

"Fine with me," said Penny.

In the middle of the night Joe awoke in terror, and the jungle noise closed in around him. Sitting up in his bed, he covered his face with his hands. Sweat had erupted on his forehead and his pulse was racing. It had been another dream … this time more vivid and more real than the others.

He remembered now what had happened. He had been riding in a cargo plane. His job was to check the supplies at various bases. Either the airplane had been targeted or an engine had failed. But they knew they were going down, and they had time to grab parachutes. Bill, the pilot, and his friend, had bailed out at the same time he had. As they dropped to the ground inside the jungle, the craft went down in flames. He'd watched as smoke and flames signaled the site of the plane crash.

When Bill found him, they were thankful they had survived without injury. They also knew they had to get as far away from the downed airplane as possible, or the Viet Cong would find them and probably kill them.

With shaky fingers, Joe found the rusty flashlight they had given him and switched it on. Then he picked up his pad of paper and pencil, which he kept underneath the cot, and began to write slowly:

> *We ran in the opposite direction. We hid when we approached a village or thought someone might see us. We had to lie low. Since we didn't have radios, there was no way to send any communication. Our mistake was bailing out without taking weapons, water or anything with us.*
> *The pilot's name was Bill. I can remember …*
> *Lieutenant Bill Crawford. My name …*

He stopped writing when he realized the dream had faded. He had hoped that he would remember his name, but he didn't. He didn't even know his own name!

Dropping the pen and note pad to the dirt floor, Joe lay back on the bed, turned on his side and wept.

Ruby had decided not to go into town with Annette and her mother later that afternoon. She was excited that Annette was going to get her driver's learning permit, and she knew Mom had to go along, to get everything signed and legal. Terry had gotten called over to the Duncans' to work, so she got to be alone in the farmhouse—something exciting in itself, even though she was so glad to have a family again. She listened to an AM radio station that played music on the little transistor radio.

"Clyde, you're so crazy." Ruby laughed as the gray kitten performed antics across the living room rug. She had made plenty of toys to keep her little cat occupied, although the kitten usually found her own entertainment from simple things like furniture legs, an empty cup, a brown paper grocery sack, and even some of Mrs. Vetter's knitting yarn.

Ruby decided to take advantage of her alone time to cut out and decorate the valentines she had planned to give to Mom, Annette and Terry. She also had planned to make one for Uncle Will. As she sat at the dining room table with a pair of scissors, some Elmer's glue, Skotch tape and red construction paper, she thought about how Mom had reacted when asked if she might want to marry Uncle Will.

"I guess that backfired," Ruby murmured to herself. She had thought it would be the perfect solution. Mrs. Vetter was widowed, and Uncle Will was a bachelor. They were close to the same age, and at Christmas they had seemed to hit it off really well. Mom always liked to cook a big dinner when her uncle came for a visit.

But Uncle Will was eccentric. Terry had said so. And it was true, after living in his small trailer in Madison, she had seen what he was like—messy, used to his routine, and just happy to stay by himself, reading his nature books, watching his small black-and-white TV, and going to work each day.

She got up and went to adjust the dial on the little transistor radio above the sink. She was sitting at the table, cutting out a big heart for Terry, when the *song* came on the radio and grabbed her attention. She always associated the song "My Dad" with her father. Ruby turned in her seat and stared at the little radio. Halfway through the tune, she suddenly sobbed and tears welled up in her blue eyes.

"My *dad* …" she wept as she held her head in her hands. "Oh, I miss him. I miss him so much." She cried, uninhibited with no one home to hear her, and even after the song ended, and the disk jockey introduced the next tune, Ruby continued to sniffle.

Finally, she got up and went into the downstairs bath-room to clean her face and see how red her eyes were. Seeing the forlorn face that belonged to her in the mirror, she almost started crying again. Instead, she wiped her face, then went back into the dining room to continue her art project. They would be back fairly soon. She had to get her valentines made before then.

A nnette and Penny rode in the back seat of Mrs. Vetter's car, elated after getting their learning permits at the community center. Audrey Duncan sat in the front passenger seat. Annette had envisioned herself getting behind the wheel and driving home, but she knew it wasn't going to happen. For one thing, she hadn't even had her first lesson, and secondly, she couldn't legally drive with other people in the car besides herself and a licensed driver who was over 18.

"Tim said he'd take me out for the first time," Penny said, "but I don't think that's going to happen for quite a while. He's been so darn busy."

"What's Tim been doing?" Mrs. Vetter asked with a

glance in the back seat. "I haven't seen him around for a while."

"Oh, he's been working with Ray and earning extra money for college," said Penny's mother.

Annette looked up. "That ... and his social life, you mean." She smiled shyly.

Penny stared at her. "Annette, he's not been going out on dates much since Christmas."

This news surprised Annette. "But I thought ..."

"No!" insisted Penny. "Tim's been really working hard for Dad. That's why he doesn't drive us to school in the mornings much. He got a pass from Mr. Edwards at school, so that he doesn't have to come to school till second hour. I thought you knew that."

Annette blinked. "No, Pen."

"Well, it doesn't matter," said Penny.

Then another thought occurred to Annette. "Does this mean he's been accepted for college?"

Mrs. Vetter perked up when she heard the question. "Oh, is Tim going to Eau Claire next fall?"

Mrs. Duncan answered her. "Not yet. He hasn't gotten his acceptance letter yet."

"Well, I hope he gets to go to college," said Mrs. Vetter. "I think he'd like Eau Claire."

"Yeah, and if he doesn't get in there, he'll probably go to Stevens Point," added Penny.

The two mothers carried on their conversation in the front seat while Annette settled back, sifting this news through her mind. Apparently she had been jumping to conclusions where Tim was concerned. She had imagined him as the lady's man, taking every opportunity to date all the older girls in the high school, and instead he was spending all his spare time on the dairy farm, earning money from his dad!

Then she thought more about the short phone conversations

she'd had with Tim recently. Had Tim been hoping Annette might invite him to the Valentines Dance? Is *that* why he'd turned down Mary Ann Maxwell? Even Penny had said to her the other night, *"Why didn't you?"* and had chastised her for not thinking she was worthy of going on a date with Penny's older brother.

Well, now she'd done it. She had invited Pete, and they were going. And she also knew that Penny really had wanted to ask Pete, but her sense of honor had kept her from it. Some Valentines Day this was going to be!

12

Ruby's Dream

When they arrived home, Annette immediately went out to the barn to do her evening chores. It wasn't quite dark yet. Ruby had already collected the eggs and closed up the chicken house for the night. Terry was still on the job over at the Duncan farm.

Annette welcomed the time she had to herself and mused over the events of her day. The science test had been difficult, but she felt a swell of pride at being prepared for once. She expected to receive a decent grade in science this semester.

Debbie Kelton was in heaven after Terry accepted her invitation to the dance. In school, their blonde friend seemed to glow with happiness, and Annette was secretly glad Terry had decided on Debbie instead of Susan Reed, who had asked him first.

As far as she knew, neither Kathy Evans nor Nancy Marshall had asked anyone. Penny, surprisingly, didn't act upset over Pete accepting Annette's invitation. But now Annette wished she could back up and do as her heart had ruled. She knew now that she should have asked Tim. After all, he was now her Number One love interest, and no matter how he had reacted to what she'd written on his birthday card, she wished now she had followed through and asked him to the dance.

"It's not fair that Pete's going to the dance with me," Annette said out loud. One of Elizabeth's black ears twitched as Annette continued to milk away, filling the pail beneath them. "I mean ... I saw it coming. Penny can deny it all she wants, but I know she really wanted to go with Pete to the Valentines Dance."

Now she didn't think she could get out of it. For one thing, it would certainly hurt Pete's feelings, and Pete was too nice to be treated that way. She could still hear Penny's voice from over a week ago, saying, "Annette ... he's *your* boyfriend!" Well, it just didn't feel like that was true any longer.

"But I'm certainly not Tim's girl either," Annette grumbled. Then she smiled to herself, remembering vividly how wonderful it had been on Christmas Eve when Tim Duncan had kissed her and held her tight, right here in this barn.

Still, she wondered how he felt about her now ... and especially after what she'd written on the card. He had wanted to talk to her about that, but somehow things had gotten messy. Controversy had developed and a misunderstanding had placed a wedge between herself and Tim.

What hurt the most, of course, was that Tim was probably going to leave for college in six months. The very idea of him leaving and never coming back made Annette depressed. Having grown up practically a member of the Duncan family since early childhood, her feelings for Tim had evolved into something she wasn't sure she knew how to handle.

That night Ruby awoke from another frightening nightmare. Fortunately, Annette was able to calm her so that no one else in the household was disturbed.

Sobbing beneath her pillow, Ruby trembled afterwards.

Annette had turned on the bedside lamp and rubbed her sister's shoulders. "Come on, Ruby," she crooned, "let it go. You're safe. I'm right here, and so is Ginger."

The collie looked up at them from his rug beside their bed. Clyde was not in the room. The kitten preferred other spots throughout the house, spending her nights roaming, exploring, and finding obscure nooks in which to rest when she grew sleepy.

"My dad …" Ruby mumbled.

"The dream was about your dad?" Annette asked gently.

"Yes." The girl peeked out from under her pillow, then relaxed as her conscious awareness resumed. "Oh, Annette, it was so vivid."

"What was it about?" asked Annette. "Do you feel like telling me? Maybe it'll help to talk about it."

Ruby rubbed her eyes, then blinked. "I saw him. He was sitting in what looked like a doorway to a tent. He was gazing out at the trees … there was so much green … so much tall grass … and the chair he was sitting on … it looked like it was wicker … or some other kind of plant material … it was something like you'd see in the summertime … or in a different … country."

"Hm," said Annette, waiting for more.

Ruby sighed, then said, "I saw tears in my dad's eyes. I walked over to him and I took his hands in mine. Oh Annette, he was so thin! He had whiskers and his face was thin too. He looked *awful!*" She shuddered. "Then he looked at me, and I know he recognized me. He said to me, 'Ruby, don't give up on me. I'm coming home.'" Then Ruby collapsed into sobs and buried her face in her hands.

"Shhhh. There now …" Annette tried her best to comfort the girl, who continued to sob, but finally grew weary as the crying subsided. As soon as Ruby settled back onto her pillow, Annette reached over and turned off the lamp. Then she lay awake for several minutes, thinking about Ruby's dream and wondering what it meant.

Wednesday morning, Mrs. Vetter reminded her family at breakfast that she would be working the afternoon and evening shift. She had left-over roast beef in the refrigerator, and they were to fend for themselves for supper.

"Do you have to work at the Duncans' again today?" Ruby asked Terry as she ate her bowl of Cream of Wheat.

"I don't think so," he replied, "but they might call me."

"Kay is learning to work in the Randts' barn," Ruby disclosed. "I told her that I milk the cow once in a while."

Annette smiled over at her sister and gave her a wink.

"Mom, do you think I can use the car Friday night?" Terry asked as he buttered a slice of toast. "It's the Valentines Dance at school."

"I know, dear," replied Mrs. Vetter as she finally sat down at the table with her cup of coffee. She smiled over at Annette. "Annette is taking Pete, and I heard you are going to the dance with Debbie Kelton. Of course, I won't have to work that night, so you can use the car."

"You'll be out on a double date!" Ruby grinned at Annette, then her brother.

"Is Pete learning to drive yet?" asked Mrs. Vetter.

Annette took a sip of orange juice and set it down. "I don't think so, Mom. He has to wait to get his learner's permit in May."

"I thought Pete was older than you," said Mrs. Vetter.

"Oh no," she replied, "but does it matter?"

"Well, of course not." Her mother laughed.

"How old are *you*, Mom?" Ruby wanted to know. She spooned more hot cereal into her mouth, then quickly reached for her napkin.

"Me?" Mrs. Vetter chuckled. "I'm old enough to know

better." She sipped her coffee.

Annette giggled. "Mom is 38 … right, Mom?"

"That's not old," said Terry. "I think Uncle Will is 45."

"My dad is 43," said Ruby. Everyone looked at her and her eyes darted from one to the other. "Well, that is … if he's still alive. He would have turned 43 on Ground Hog Day."

The others were silent and continued to eat their breakfast. Annette sensed tension in the room, all of a sudden.

"Do you wanna know *why* I know Dad's alive?" Ruby spoke up unexpectedly.

"Yes, please tell us," encouraged Mrs. Vetter.

"My dream told me last night," said Ruby and a smile spread across her cheeks. "I saw him, and he told me that he's coming *home*."

Terry stared at the girl, moved by her words. "But Ruby, it was only a dream."

She shook her head. "No, it was different this time. I really did see him, and he spoke to me. I heard his voice."

"She did wake up in the night," Annette said in defense of her sister. "She told me about it then."

"Well," said Mrs. Vetter, reaching for the jar of Welch's grape jelly to spread on her toast. "Sometimes our dreams can be tricky. It's not unusual to dream about loved ones who have left us."

Terry pushed his chair back and carried his dishes to the sink. "We'd better hurry, Annette. Penny will be here any minute."

The topic had been closed purposely. Annette finished eating, then ran upstairs to finish getting ready for school. She was a little worried about Ruby interpreting the dream about her dad. She knew that, according to the authorities, Bob Foley was presumed dead. She knew Ruby was having trouble accepting that fact, which was why the dreams plagued her. Unfortunately, the nightmares were coming back. Annette had hoped that having Clyde in Ruby's life would make things better for the girl.

As if in response, Annette walked into the upstairs bathroom and discovered the little gray kitten curled up inside the sink. "You stinker!" she cried, then burst out laughing. "That's no place to sleep." She reached for her toothbrush and the kitten scrambled up and jumped to the floor. Still chuckling, Annette turned on the faucet and squeezed some Colgate onto her brush.

One afternoon after a couple of weeks had passed, Kim-Ly showed up in the company of a little scrawny gentleman, whom she introduced to Joe as he was finishing the broth Kim-Ly's mother had fed him for lunch. The two exchanged words in Vietnamese, but then the little old man squatted in front of where Joe sat, next to his bed, and he looked into Joe's eyes with a kind smile.

"Hullo. American?"

Surprised, Joe nodded and set his empty bowl next to the chair. Kim-Ly stepped back and folded her hands in front of her, encouraging him with a smile to answer the old man.

"Uh … yes. You understand English?"

The old man nodded, then pointed a short, stubby finger at himself. "I am called Sinh. I learn English, though not very good."

"It's a pleasure to meet you, Sinh." Joe offered his thin hand, and Sinh embraced it gently.

"You have name?" the old man asked.

"I … can't remember it," he confessed. "I am trying very hard to remember."

Sinh communicated this to Kim-Ly, then turned his attention back to Joe. "She call you Joe."

"Yes," he said with a smile. "I know, but it's not my real name."

"You are … soldier? American, yes?"

"U.S. Air Force," he revealed. "My cargo plane crashed. The trouble is, I don't know much about what happened before or after that event. It's coming back to me in pieces."

Again, Sinh communicated to Kim-Ly what he'd said. She told him something else.

"We are working to get you safely out of country," Sinh explained. "We do not know who to trust. Your life is in much danger here."

"Yes, I know that," he said. "And I am very grateful to Kim-Ly and her parents, and also Dr. Nguyen, for the care they have shown me. I know they risk much by my being here."

"Kim-Ly say no I.D. on you when you arrive at hospital."

He shrugged. "I have no idea why. I believe those tags were taken from me." Then he thought of something to say. "If it is of any help, I do remember the man I was with. His name was First Lieutenant Bill Crawford. I guess you already know … he didn't make it."

Sinh nodded and translated what he'd said to Kim-Ly. He then explained all that he could remember about the plane crash, which the old man repeated in Vietnamese.

"Do you know how to contact any Americans?" Joe asked.

"I must work on this." Sinh started to get up. He reached over and patted Joe on the thigh. "If necessary, I will return. We must be careful. Viet Cong are everywhere. Nobody can be trusted."

The old man and Kim-Ly left. Joe felt stimulated by the conversation with Sinh. He was just frustrated that he couldn't explain his situation. All he'd been able to remember was the bright round face of his daughter. Yes, he knew she was his daughter. As for the older woman's face from his dream … it had to have been his wife. Those two had been members of his family. Who else could they be?

And he also knew that they had no idea if he was alive or dead.

13

February Thaw

The next morning as Annette, Penny and Terry walked to the bus stop, Annette felt Spring in the air. "Hey, are we having a February thaw?" she asked. The sun was out with clear blue skies, and the snow seemed to be melting from its gritty appearance. The pavement on the road was becoming more visible except where trees kept it shady.

"Wow, it feels like it," said Terry, who had already unzipped the top of his parka.

"See? You can't always depend on those ground hogs," said Penny.

"We usually get a thaw every January," remarked Annette, "but this year it was cold the whole month."

"Spring will officially be here in less than five weeks," said Terry.

"Well, it can't come soon enough in my opinion," said Penny.

"Yeah." Annette laughed, then said, "But then it will be Mud Season."

"Gee, you're right," said Penny. "Cheeze is already getting muddy. Mom says I have to keep a pail of water and a towel by the door, and clean his feet before he comes into the house."

"I do that with Ginger at times," added Annette.

"Has the kitten been outside yet?" Penny asked Terry.

"No," he said. "Ruby keeps Clyde in the house. She's turning out to be quite the eccentric cat."

When they reached the bus stop, the bus arrived only a minute later. Pete beckoned to them from the back seat, his eyes wide with excitement. "I've got news," he told them.

Slipping into the seat in front of the boys, Annette and Penny turned to face Pete. "By the look on your face, I'd say it's not good news," said Annette.

"What's wrong, Pete?" asked Penny.

Ruffling his hair, Pete looked at all three of them and said, "Those rustlers are back in the area. My dad was down at Browns' Store yesterday and Mr. Brown told him that a coupl'a farmers out on the east side of the county had some animals stolen."

"When?" Penny's green eyes widened with worry.

"Earlier this week," said Pete. "You're friends with Lisa Kowalski, right? From FFA?"

"Yeah," said Annette, encouraging him to continue.

"Well, my dad said Mr. Kowalski lost about a dozen of his cattle."

Terry whistled. Annette's and Penny's mouths dropped open.

Pete added, "And there's a horse farm down the road from them. They lost a number of their stock as well."

"Horses?" Penny looked alarmed.

"Oh my gosh," Annette muttered. "I wonder if it was Fred Pruett's horse farm."

Pete nodded his head. "That's it ... that's what he said — Mr. Pruett — and they think the thieves wiped out his wife's chicken house as well."

"That's horrible," cried Penny.

"How does anyone get away with stealing livestock?"

asked Terry. "I mean … it's not like you can hide big animals like that for long."

"You're right," said Pete, "but it happens. Dad told me the sheriff thought the culprits had cleared out of the area, but apparently this gang is not too smart."

"Well, how did they …" Annette trailed off.

"They manage to get them when they're out to pasture," explained Pete. "Lisa's parents have a big spread, so their cattle are all over the place. But Mr. Brown told my dad they're sending patrols out from now on, especially at night."

"If they are stealing chickens, I'd better lock the coop with a padlock," said Annette, very concerned.

"I'm pretty sure Ginger would alert us if anyone came around," Terry tried to assure her.

"Well, I sure hope they catch them!" Penny was fired up. She looked at Pete and asked, "You didn't lose any more animals, did you?"

"Nope," Pete replied and caught the sympathy on her face. "But it makes me want to stand guard."

Annette turned away to stare out the window of the bus. She had caught the look that Pete and Penny exchanged just then. A pang of guilt hit her as the conversation in the back seat pattered on. She wondered what she was going to do about the situation she'd gotten herself into with asking Pete to the Valentines Dance. It was so obvious that Penny and Pete were—despite not displaying it openly—becoming more fond of one another.

The morning dragged, as usual, at school. When they had gone through the lunch line, Annette and Penny sought out Lisa Kowalski, who was sitting at a table with a couple of her senior friends. She smiled and invited the two of them to join their table.

"We heard that the cattle rustlers came back," said Annette. "Oh, Lisa, I'm so sorry."

"Yes, I know," said the tall, dark-haired girl with glasses. "My parents are really angry."

"Can you tell us anything more?" asked Penny.

"Not really," said Lisa. "The sheriff was out, of course, and they're investigating. But the worst of it was our neighbor, Mr. Pruett. He lost three horses."

Annette explained how she and Ruby had gone with Uncle Will out to the Pruett farm two weeks ago. "He must have had some horses out," she guessed. "When we were there for a visit, most of them were inside the stable."

"Well, with this warmer weather, I'm sure he didn't give it a thought keeping them out," said Lisa.

The conversation started to drift toward other things as Annette ate her lunch. She discreetly looked around the cafeteria until her eyes found Tim, who was sitting at a far table in the corner, joined by Terry. The rowdy senior boys were at the next table, but Tim and Terry appeared to be having a private and more serious discussion. She involved herself back into the conversation at Lisa's table, not wanting to make herself obvious where Tim was concerned.

One day, a month or so after the old man, Sinh, had come to visit Joe, another foreigner was treated at Dr. Nguyen's jungle hospital. When Kim-Ly tried to explain this to Joe, he naturally did not understand her words. But he knew something significant had happened because of the excitement in her voice and the way her parents reacted after she'd come home and told them.

By this time, Joe had gained back more of his strength, and his bones had healed so that he could write better, for one thing. He found that writing down his thoughts, and particularly his nocturnal dreams, helped him in his challenge to remember his past. Bits and pieces emerged every now and then, to the point where he recalled more of what had happened after the plane crash.

He and Bill, the pilot, had suffered for a couple of weeks on a strenuous trek through the steaming jungle. Usually, they rested and stayed hidden during daylight, and ventured farther at night when no one could spot them. The heat and humidity, along with the mosquitoes and snakes, added to their discomfort, and it was difficult finding enough water, let alone any food. They were beginning to wear down.

Exhausted, the two men practically stumbled into a small settlement of farmers. They knew it was risky to reveal themselves, even to a simple farmer and his wife and children in a rice paddy, yet they were on their last legs. The family took in the two Americans, sheltering them in their hut and giving them rice and dirty water. Before dusk on the following day, both men became violently ill, probably from the polluted water and raw meat they'd been fed.

Joe remembered the awful sickness and fever, but worse came the next day. Viet Cong had been alerted, and he and Bill were dragged off by five ruthless men, who took the Americans to their prison camp. At that point, Joe recalled waking up in a filthy pen beside Bill. Both men had been stripped of their clothing and any identifying trinkets. They were given rags to wear, and the Viet Cong beat them and forced them to do slave labor. They were already sick and weak, yet if they did not comply with their captors, they knew death would follow.

How long this went on, he couldn't say. At one point, they had tortured the two of them almost to the point of death, then abandoned them, assuming they were dead. Joe remembered the two of them waking up in a pit of filth and corpses. He was conscious enough to drag his friend along with him out of the pit, even though he suffered from his wounds and wasn't sure how far they could get.

Joe's memory was unreliable concerning the next few

days as he and Bill trudged slowly through the jungle, hiding, fighting for survival, expecting death to come at any moment, either from the Viet Cong or from the elements themselves.

He remembered slipping on a bank near a river or stream and injuring himself further. He figured that was probably the point where he blanked out everything in his mind. Bill helped him from that point on, but by the time they came within sight of Dr. Nguyen's hospital, both of them had exhausted themselves and they collapsed on the path.

Joe read what he'd written on his notepad, then added:

That's all I know. I still don't know my name. Bill kept calling me "Major." I keep dreaming about my family. I do have a family in the States. A daughter and a son. Yes, a good-looking young man with blond hair like his sister. The woman … my wife? I see her face and I know she is my wife … but I get a troubled feeling whenever I think of her. I wish I knew their names. I wish I knew where they live. What do they possibly believe about me? Is there anyone searching for me?

That night after dark, Kim-Ly and Dr. Nguyen came for him and walked him over to the hospital, half a mile away, on the outskirts of the little village. They whispered and were constantly looking over their shoulders as if they were afraid of someone seeing them. Joe remained silent, wondering what awaited him. Obviously, there was a good reason … or perhaps he had been discovered and his life was again in danger.

As the hospital, with a burning candle in one of the windows, came into sight, he took a deep breath and decided he would have to be brave and trust these two Vietnamese healers. His fate was in their hands.

When Annette got home from school that afternoon, she looked up the number of Fred Pruett in the phone book and dialed the number of the Pruett horse farm. Lucy answered the phone after three rings.

"Hello, Mrs. Pruett," said Annette. "You probably don't remember me. I'm Annette Vetter. I came out to your farm a couple of weeks ago with Will Knutson, a friend of your husband's."

Lucy grew excited. "Oh, of course I remember you!" Then she fell into a storm of tears. "Have you heard what happened? Three of our horses are gone—*gone! And my chickens … all* of them … somebody came and swooped them up in the night. I just can't believe this happened!" She broke into sobs.

"Yes, I heard about it," Annette said quietly, and waited for the hysterical woman to calm down. "I thought I would call and see if there is anything we can do to help."

At the other end of the line, Mrs. Pruett blew her nose into a hanky, then said, "Oh, that is so kind and so thoughtful of you, Annette." She spoke away from the telephone, "Fred, it's Will's niece on the phone …"

"I'm not his…" Annette started to say.

Then, Fred Pruett came on the line. "Annette? Thank you for calling. I'm sorry … my wife is upset."

Annette heard him direct Lucy into another room. "Can you tell me what happened?" she asked when he was back on the line.

"Rustlers, that's what," said Fred Pruett. "They must have come while Lucy and I were at the Grange meeting last evening. They were having a pot luck and a lot of the farmers were there."

"Gosh," said Annette.

"Anyway," said Fred, "when we got home, I went to the stables to check things out for the night. Lucy hadn't closed up the chickens yet, so she went out at the same time."

"How late did you get home?" asked Annette.

"Oh, it must have been nine or nine-thirty," said Mr. Pruett.

"And what then?"

"Well, all the horses in the barn were all right. Thank goodness for that."

"Sundown too?" asked Annette.

"Why, yes," he replied. "Sundown is all right. But … it wasn't until Lucy came screaming into the barn about the chickens being gone that we grew suspicious. I went out to the coop and the chicken yard with her, and we saw tracks and footprints … someone had driven in while we were gone, and … I don't know how they managed to do it … but they took the whole flock … rooster, hens, chicks … every bird!"

Annette didn't know what to tell him.

"Then," resumed Fred, "I saddled up and rode out to the pastures, and that's when I discovered three horses were gone. They didn't get all of them … I had about twelve horses outside the barn yesterday. But there was evidence of a truck being in there by the gate. Again, I don't know how they rounded them up. But they got away with it!"

"That's terrible," said Annette. "Do you have any idea who might have gotten in and done this?"

"No, ma'am." Fred Pruett sniffed. "Of course, the sheriff and his deputies have been out. They said this happened to the Kowalski farm down the road."

"Yes, Lisa's my friend," said Annette.

"Well, thank you for your concern, young lady," Fred continued. "I'm afraid there's not anything you can do, really." He moved the receiver away from his mouth and she heard him say, "Lucy, calm down …"

"I hope the rustlers get caught," Annette told Mr. Pruett when he came back on the line. "If I hear anything more, I'll call you."

"I'd appreciate that," said Fred, "and it was very nice of you to call us."

After the conversation ended, Annette put on her farm

coat and went out to do her chores. Ruby had gone over to Duncans' with Terry, who was working in their dairy barn. Ruby got along well with Karen, Penny's six-year-old sister, and Annette felt suddenly vulnerable being alone.

She had never felt uneasy before, and she had stayed alone many times while Mrs. Vetter had worked the evening shift at the hospital. But with all the trouble in the area with people's livestock being stolen, she imagined all kinds of frightening scenarios as she first checked on the chickens, which were already roosting inside their coop for the night. She went ahead and put out some feed for them, then closed them up for the night.

Stepping outside in the growing darkness, Annette sighed and knelt down to pet Ginger, who stood at her side, calmly cocking his head at her as if to say, *"What are you worried about? I'm here to watch out for you."* After giving his red head and white collie mane a good petting, she led the way to the barn, where Elizabeth and Alice were waiting patiently to be milked.

She noticed the difference in the air. Even though it was still February, it was getting warmer. The sun was setting a few minutes later each evening. It had been a long, cold winter in Wisconsin and now Spring was just around the corner. Valentines Day was in two days … and yet she felt she was taking the wrong boy to the dance.

14

Intruders

Annette had just finished up with the milking and was storing the milk in the cooling room of the barn when she heard Ginger barking. She quickly ran out to find him whining at the door and scratching to be let out.

"What is it, Ginger?" Annette glanced around, then cautiously went to open the door and let the dog out. The moment he could squeeze through the doorway, the collie bounded out and then stopped, his ears pricked and his head turning right, then left. A growl came from his throat.

Annette could see that dusk had come. The sky was indigo in the west through the treetops. Ginger started sniffing the ground and walked toward the chicken house, which was to the east. Just as she took a few steps toward her dog, she noticed a swift movement in the direction of the woods behind the chicken yard. Ginger let out a series of barking and took off toward that area.

Seized with a sudden fear, Annette was hesitant at first to follow her dog. Her heart pounded as she strained to see through the darkness. She carried a pen light in her coat pocket, so reached in and pulled it out. Ginger ran toward the woods when she flicked on the light and shone it in his direction.

Annette gasped when she saw a dark figure running through the trees. Ginger had seen whoever it was and had taken after him. Annette quickly shut the barn door behind her without turning off the lights inside, then walked as far as the chicken coop and stopped.

Everything was quiet for a few seconds. Ginger was in the woods, and every once in a while she heard him barking. She wondered if she should follow him, but she was afraid. What if she was accosted? Her mind immediately turned to the livestock rustlers in the area. Had they been on the Vetters' property? Was there anyone else around, perhaps watching her right now?

"Ginger! Come on!" Annette yelled, her voice echoing in the growing darkness.

The collie continued to bark in the woods, and then Annette distinctly heard the roar of a truck engine. Someone had been parked off the road on the east side of their property. She bravely moved toward the chicken coop, shining her narrow beam of light to see if anything there had been disturbed. Everything was quiet. Apparently Ginger's barking had interrupted the intruder's intentions.

A couple of minutes later, she saw the faint headlights through the distant tree trunks and watched as they moved down the road toward town. She called Ginger again and this time the collie bounded out of the woods toward her, excited, with his hackles up.

Annette turned and ran to the house with Ginger at her heels. She was out of breath when she got inside. Ginger came in and paced throughout the rooms, still worked up. As soon as she hung up her coat, Annette ran into the dining room and dialed the Duncans' phone number.

Penny answered as Annette was still trying to catch her breath.

"What's wrong?" Penny sounded alarmed. "Annette, is

everything all right?"

"No," said Annette. "Pen, please tell Terry to come home."

"Annette, what happened?" Penny demanded.

"There was … there was someone outside," she panted. "Ginger heard them when I was out milking. I saw someone in the woods. And then I heard a truck start up, and I saw the lights as it drove away."

"Oh my gosh, Annette!"

In the background, Annette heard Ruby ask, "Is Annette okay?"

"I think they're almost finished out in the barn," explained Penny. "I'll run out right now and tell them."

"I'm scared," Annette admitted. "I had a strange feeling earlier … I guess all this talk about rustlers has me worked up."

"No, Annette, I don't blame you," said Penny. "Okay, I'm going out to the barn right now." She hung up, and Annette placed the phone back in its cradle.

Clyde had wandered into the room and Ginger touched his long collie nose to the kitten's head. The little gray cat rolled on her back and playfully struck a paw out at her canine companion.

By the time Annette had gone upstairs to change clothes and wash up, she heard Terry come home. When she hurried downstairs, she was met by not only Terry and Ruby, but Tim … all of them looking very concerned and worried about her.

"Penny told us what happened," said Terry, unzipping his parka.

Ruby's blue eyes were wide with fear, and Tim hung back by the door with his hands in his jacket pockets. His eyes met Annette's with equal concern.

"Annette, can you tell us what happened?" Tim asked.

She told them what she had heard and seen, and the two

boys looked at one another. Then Tim nudged Terry and said, "Let's go check it out."

Terry gave Annette a nod, then started to follow Tim out the door.

"Where are you going?" asked Ruby, her voice shaking.

"Grab a flashlight," said Tim.

Terry went to the utility drawer in the kitchen and pulled out a large flashlight. "We'll be right back," he told his sister with a small smile. "We're just gonna check the woods by the road."

"I'll warm up some supper," Annette called after them. "Ruby, will you help me?"

After the boys went outside to look around, Ruby helped Annette get out the left-over roast beef Mrs. Vetter had cooked that week. Preparing their supper helped ease their preoccupied minds, and Annette tried to comfort the younger girl by asking her about her day.

"Did you have fun over at Duncans'?"

"Yes," said Ruby, getting the silverware out of the drawer. "Penny and I played games with Karen. Mrs. Duncan went to a meeting, which is why Penny didn't come over too."

"I see," said Annette, understanding that someone had to stay with the six-year-old. "Well, I'm glad you enjoy Karen."

"Little kids are really fun." Ruby smiled as she set the table. Annette noticed she had set an extra place for Tim. "I like being around Kay's brothers and sisters too."

"Maybe you'll grow up to be a teacher or something," said Annette.

"Maybe."

The food was warmed up and everything was ready for them when the two boys came back into the house.

"Please stay and have something to eat with us," Annette said to Tim with a smile.

When he started to protest, Terry coaxed him. "Aw, come

on … my mom's roast beef is out of this world."

"Roast beef, huh?" Tim grinned, then took off his jacket and set it on the hook over Annette's farm coat.

"Wash up first," said Annette. "Ruby, get the bread and butter out."

"Mom made homemade bread yesterday," Ruby reported, "and is it ever good!"

Annette was slicing the bread onto a wooden board when Terry and Tim came out of the downstairs bathroom after cleaning up. They took their seats at the table and Annette and Ruby joined them.

"Did you find anything?" Annette asked Terry.

"Yeah, there were definitely tracks," he replied with a glance at Tim, who sat quietly, waiting. "Both footprints and a large vehicle," he added.

"Do you think it was those rustlers?" asked Annette.

"There's a good possibility," said Tim, "but we can't jump to conclusions."

"Well, the bottom line is somebody was on the property," said Terry. "Somebody who wasn't supposed to be here … and he gave my sister a heck of a scare."

"If it hadn't been for Ginger," said Annette, reaching for the bowl of peas, "it's hard to tell what would have happened."

"Well, until the sheriff gets these thieves rounded up, I don't want you to be here alone." Tim stared at Annette with concern.

Looking up at his face, Annette's eyes were caught in his gaze. Her heart did a pitter-patter until she finally cleared her throat and looked away.

"He's right, Annette," said Terry. Ruby handed him a slice of bread and he reached for the butter dish.

"Can we talk about something else now?" asked Ruby. Her eyes were watering and her lip trembled.

"Yes, we will definitely change the subject." Annette smiled at her little sister, then passed the plate of beef in Tim's direction.

"Valentines Day is in two days," Ruby announced cheerfully.

At the mention of that reminder, Annette's throat swelled with emotion. She purposely avoided looking at Tim, but she could tell he was staring at her. She could feel his eyes on her.

"Well, what have you got planned for Valentines Day, Ruby?" Terry asked as he buttered his bread.

"Tomorrow Mom is letting me bake valentine cookies," the girl announced. "I'm going to make a whole bunch of them and give them away to my friends at school." She seemed pleased with her decision, and her mood had quickly shifted from the idea of an intruder to the fun she had planned.

"You mean cookies in the shape of hearts?" asked Terry.

"What else?" Annette chuckled, but then caught Tim's gaze again and felt herself blushing.

Terry and Ruby did most of the talking while they ate. Annette wasn't paying much attention to what anybody was saying. She suddenly wanted more than anything to take Tim aside and have a talk with him. She needed to know, once and for all, if he resented her for having asked Pete to the dance. She thought maybe after they finished, she could say she was going out to the barn because she'd left the lights on … and Tim would probably speak up and say he'd go with her. That was her chance.

The boys finished their plates first and waited patiently for the girls. Ruby had talked so much at the table, she still had a lot of food left on her plate.

"Thanks for the meal," Tim said suddenly and flashed Annette a smile. "It was delicious."

Annette took that as her cue to stand up and clear off their plates. "It was nothing," she said and reached for his plate, then let Terry hand her his.

"Don't act so innocent," Terry said to Annette. He turned to Tim and said, "She's a great cook."

Embarrassed, Annette made excuses. "Well, Mom worked so much all those years, I had to cook for myself ... or starve." She tried to laugh, but it came out as a nervous cackle as she took the dirty dishes to the sink.

"I'd better get back home," said Tim and stood up.

Annette was turning to ask if he'd go with her out to the barn, but just then the telephone rang. She slipped into the dining room to answer it.

"Annette?" It was Penny. "Is Tim still there?"

"Yes ... he had supper with us."

"Oh. Well, Dad said he needs to come home. There's something he needs him to do."

"Oh, all right," said Annette.

After she hung up, Tim already had on his jacket and was telling Terry goodbye. "That was Penny," she started to say.

"Yeah, I know," said Tim. "My dad's waiting." He nodded at her and smiled once again. "Thanks again, Annette."

"You're ... you're welcome, Tim." She didn't want him to leave, but she knew he had to. "Bye."

"See ya," he said to the three of them, and then he was out the door, headed for his Chevelle that was parked in the driveway.

Annette stood at the kitchen window and watched him get into the car, start it up and back down to the road.

"Hey, I think you left the lights on in the barn," Terry called to her and she turned to face him.

"Yeah, I know."

"I'll go out and turn them off," he said.

"Okay. Thanks, Terry." Annette went to the sink and began to draw hot water.

"I'll dry." Ruby stood with a grin on her face, then pouted.

"Annette … why are you sad?"

"Sad?" Annette immediately perked up and smiled at her sister. "I'm not sad."

Ruby placed her hands on her hips and rolled her eyes. "Tim really likes you," she told Annette.

Surprised, Annette's mouth dropped open. "Why would you say that?"

"Oh, Annette, it's so obvious." She giggled.

Annette grabbed the detergent bottle from under the sink and squeezed some soap into the water filling the sink. She didn't say anything.

Ruby wouldn't give it up. "So, Annette, why did you ask Pete Randt to the dance instead of Tim?"

Annette sighed, then smiled at the younger girl. "It's a mystery to me too, Ruby," she replied.

"Yes, and I know how much you love mysteries." Suddenly, she gasped. "I forgot to feed Clyde!"

"Oh, you'd better do that," said Annette, "and while you're at it, would you feed Ginger too?"

Ruby ran to the cupboard where the pet food was, and Annette slouched over the sink, the soothing hot water on her hands soaking away the hurt that was in her heart. She had failed to let Tim know … and there was nothing to do now except follow through with going to the dance with Pete.

In the candle-lit hospital room, Joe stood facing the man who lay on the cot he had once occupied. Kim-Ly and the doctor stepped back and waited. Before him was a man like himself, tall and slender, but with reddish hair and a handlebar red mustache. The man propped himself up to stare at the man facing him.

"They told me you were here," he said and reached out a hairy wrist for Joe to shake. The man had a British accent. "They said an American had come to their hospital. They are hoping that somehow I can help you."

Doctor Nguyen pushed a stool over and motioned for Joe to sit, which he did.

Not exactly sure how to react to this stranger, he paused a few seconds and then spoke. "Can you help me?" he asked.

"Well, it depends, friend. I understand you have forgotten your name and where you came from."

Joe nodded and sighed.

"Military, I presume …"

"Air Force," said Joe. "I'm a major. That's all I remember … besides my pilot, Bill Crawford … a first lieutenant."

"Jolly good." The man grinned, then settled back against the cot with his hands behind his head. "That's a start at least."

"And who are you?" asked Joe.

"Lloyd Lovingood, at your service," said the Englishman.

"Please tell me how you arrived here," Joe said, suspicious and untrusting.

"Well, I am not in service to my country, nor any other for that matter. But that is neither here nor there, my friend. I had a little run-in a day or two ago with our friends, the Viet Cong …"

"They are *not* my friends, sir," Joe emphasized with a frown. "They nearly killed me, and they tortured us before leaving us for dead in a pit full of corpses. Bill died here at this hospital." He glanced over at the doctor, then back to the man on the cot. "And so, Mr. Lloyd Lovingood, you're going to have to convince me that you won't betray me. If you're planning to turn me over to the authorities, then this is where we part company … and that includes these gracious people who took me in." He nodded at Kim-Ly and the doctor, who—not understanding—smiled and nodded their heads.

Lloyd Lovingood laughed, then fell into a coughing spell. Recovering himself quickly, he looked Joe in the eye and said, "My business is in commodities, my friend. I have no interest in your politics nor your wars, except where it affects my profit margin."

"Meaning … what is it you deal in?" Joe was afraid to ask, but he had to know what this man's business was and why he was in the jungles of Vietnam.

"None of that matters really," said the Englishman. "What matters is that we need to get you out of here, before you are discovered and slain. I may be the man who can help you."

15

The Clue in the Snow

The next morning was crisp and clear. Annette went out to the barn to do her chores earlier than usual, so she could look around in the east woods before breakfast. Ginger stayed beside her as she emerged from the barn and watched the sun starting to come up through the trees.

"Come on, Ginger, let's do a little investigating," Annette said as she gathered the collar of her coat together. The air was frosty as she began walking in the direction of the chicken yard. The rooster crowed.

Suddenly, her collie left her side and padded over to the side of the barn. Ginger began sniffing the ground underneath a window. Curious, Annette wandered over and saw footprints in the snow. Ginger looked up at her and panted as if to say, "Look here."

She bent down and saw large boot prints that appeared fresh. The prints came from the chicken yard and another set led into the woods just north of the chicken house. Apparently someone had come to the barn last evening while she was inside. They had looked into the window, then fled through the woods behind the chicken yard.

Annette followed the prints only twenty yards before

they got mingled among other prints in the snow that had been there before, made by herself and family members. But it frightened her a little to believe that the intruder had actually been peering in at her through a window when she was inside, milking the cows, or maybe after she had finished and was putting the milk away in the storage cooler. That's when Ginger had started barking.

With a sigh, Annette stood up and started in the direction she remembered seeing the fleeing figure escape through the woods. Ginger trotted a few feet in front of her and seemed to know which way to go. She could see Terry's and Tim's footprints, where they had entered the woods, and she followed them all the way to the edge of the road.

Sure enough, tire tracks indicated that a vehicle had been parked just off Ogden Road on the Vetters' side. She looked around and found nothing else to investigate, so decided to turn around and go back to the house. First, she'd stop at the chicken coop and release the birds for the day. Opening the chickens in the morning was now Ruby's chore, but Annette knew her sister wouldn't mind.

She was relieved to find everything as it usually was inside the chicken coop. The hens flocked out the door into their fenced yard, while Annette checked their water and added some mash to their feed pans. The rooster waited for his hens to go outside, then followed, leaving only three hens that were still sitting in their nesting boxes, laying their eggs.

Annette gathered up a half dozen or so warm eggs and pocketed them carefully, then stepped outside into full sunshine. She latched shut the top half of the chicken door, which allowed the birds to come and go through the bottom half. Then, as she walked outside the fenced area and made sure the gate was closed, something shiny caught her eye.

She didn't think much of it at first, but as she started toward the house, she stopped and turned around. She retraced her steps until she caught sight again of the object that was reflecting sunlight on the snowy ground next to the chicken house. Ginger had already wandered over to the house and was waiting for her in front of the porch.

Annette bent down and reached for what had caught her eye. She picked up a medallion tied with a thin piece of nylon string. The object was made of a shiny copper-colored metal, about the size of a silver dollar. She turned it over and examined it in her hand.

"What is this?" she mumbled to herself, turning it over, then back again. She had to squint to make out the printing on the face side of the medallion. After clearing some dirt off it, she read:

1st Place Bronco Riding, Jackson County Fair, July 1968

Annette carried it to the house and when she got inside, Mrs. Vetter was already up, preparing breakfast at the stove. Annette emptied her pockets and put the fresh eggs in a carton in the refrigerator.

"Good morning," said Mrs. Vetter. "You'd better see if Ruby is out of bed. I called her five minutes ago."

"I will, Mom." Annette hung up her farm coat, and with the medallion in her hand, rushed upstairs. Terry was still in the bathroom, so she went to the girls' bedroom, where Ruby had just made the bed and was deciding what to wear to school that day.

"Hi, Annette."

"Look what I found." Annette showed her sister the medallion.

"What is it?" The girl touched it, but looked puzzled.

"I think it's a medal somebody won at the county fair last summer." Annette explained how she had found it outside the chicken yard.

"Who does it belong to?" asked Ruby.

"I don't know," said Annette. "Oh … I wanted to tell you that I already took care of the chickens."

Ruby grinned. "Okay. Thanks."

Annette went to her closet to pick out the dress she was going to wear today. Just then, she heard Terry coming out of the upstairs bathroom. She rushed in to rinse off the medallion in the sink. She couldn't find any name or other identifying mark, but she had a strong suspicion that this medallion may have been dropped by the person who had visited their farm last night.

Naturally, Mrs. Vetter was concerned when she learned about the excitement the evening before. She listened to Annette's story while they sat at the breakfast table. Bacon and eggs and homemade toasted bread were this morning's meal, with Ginger in his spot in the corner of the kitchen, watching everyone's actions as he lay with his front paws in front of his long collie nose.

"Well, I hope those thieves get caught soon," said Mrs. Vetter. "People can't make a living raising livestock when they get stolen in the middle of the night. And how many cattle did the Randts lose?"

"Six, I think," Annette answered.

"Even one animal is crucial," Terry added. "They're hardly able to make ends meet as it is."

"Well, I don't think the Duncans have lost any animals," said Ruby, reaching for another slice of bacon.

"That's probably because they usually keep their cows inside the barns this time of year," said Annette.

"Mr. Duncan is reluctant to let them out to pasture, even though it's getting warmer," added Terry.

"It sure didn't feel any warmer out this morning," Annette remarked. She had carefully placed the copper medallion into her purse before coming down to breakfast. Ruby was the only one who knew about it. Annette had not told her how she thought it might have been dropped by an intruder.

Later, when she was riding to school on the bus, Annette and Penny sat in the seat ahead of Terry and Pete, and Annette told her friend about the footprints. Then she pulled the medallion out of her purse to show Penny.

"Wow … Annette … I think this could be a clue."

"I agree," said Annette.

"Maybe we should tell somebody," said Penny.

"I don't have any proof." Annette shrugged as Penny examined the object more carefully.

"Still … this could help the police find out who was on your property, and maybe even lead to the rustlers."

Pete leaned over the back of the seat and said, "What is that you've got there?"

"Annette found a clue," Penny told him, holding up the medallion.

Terry had just finished telling Pete about the evening's excitement, and he leaned over to see the object as well. "Where did you find that?" he asked.

"Outside the chicken coop," said Annette.

"It's from the Jackson County fair," said Pete.

Terry took his turn looking at it, then returned it to Annette. "You need to tell the sheriff," he said.

"That's what I told her," said Penny.

"But what if it's nothing?" asked Annette. But she could see that all three of them were convinced it had something to do with the livestock rustlers, and at the very least, the person who had trespassed last night.

"Okay. You're right," said Annette.

"I'll walk with you to the office when we get to school," said Pete with a smile.

Annette smiled back at him, but all she could think about was how she had failed to have that talk with Tim last night, before he drove home. She hadn't planned on talking to Pete first … but it was going to be now or never.

A couple more weeks passed and the jungle was swelter-ing. Joe had returned to the hut attached to Kim-Ly's parent's house, where he continued to improve. His wounds were healing and he was starting to regain his strength. He was grateful to the doctor and Kim-Ly and her parents, who went to a lot of trouble to keep him clean with boiled, treated drinking water and enough food, which he never questioned.

Joe's dreams continued each night. He often awoke in a sweat, breathing hard, after reliving the plane crash and the trek through unforgiving jungle terrain with his pilot, Bill Crawford. Then he also had flashes of memory from their capture by the Viet Cong, which always left him terrorized.

Once in a while, he dreamed of his life before the war, "snapshots" of what he presumed to be his family back in the States. But he could still not recall his name or where he had lived.

That same week, in the middle of the night, he was gently awakened by Kim-Ly's father and another man, whom he soon discovered was the British hospital patient, Lloyd Lovingood.

"We must be extremely quiet," Lovingood whispered as he helped Joe dress and prepare to travel. "No one must see us leave the village."

Joe was pretty sure no one else knew he was there, but he asked the man, "Where are you taking me?"

"You'll know soon enough, my good man," Lovingood replied. "I have two local guides who will help us get to the river."

"How far is the river?"

"Three days travel on foot, if we are not captured first."

Joe shuddered as he slipped on his sandals that Kim-Ly had provided for him, along with the clothes they had made for him. He wanted to know what their chances were of getting there safely, but decided it was better not to ask.

The first bell rang. Annette sighed as she cradled her purse and her French book, then slammed the locker door. She had left a message about the medallion with the sheriff's office. The call had taken longer than she thought it would, and Pete had left the office to go to his locker before his first class. She realized she wasn't going to be able to talk to Pete about the Valentines Dance till later.

Throughout French, which she had first hour, Annette found it hard to concentrate on Miss Gable's conversation. Then in Art, which she had second hour, she began to dwell on what she had to say to Pete as she worked on her second clay project. The last thing she wanted to do was hurt Pete's feelings after he'd been so nice to her the last couple of months.

"Pete, I need to talk to you," she imagined herself saying if they were standing together in the hall during Break. As her fingers worked the wet clay in front of her, Annette planned out the words she would use.

He would probably smile and ask, "What is it you want to tell me, Annette?"

And then she'd take a deep breath, look up at him and boldly proclaim, "I believe Penny really wants to ask you to the Valentines Dance, and so I am *un*-inviting you."

No, no, no! Annette frowned as she formed her clay into an animal. She knew that was the wrong thing to say. Instead, she might say, "Pete, I really want you to know that you're terrific. I do like you. *But …*"

Then he'd look worried and his smile would vanish.

Bravely, she would take another deep breath and spit it out. "Pete, I think you should go to the Valentines Dance with Penny. She really wanted to be the one to ask you."

Then Pete would protest and say, "Wait! *You* asked me. Penny didn't ask me to the dance, *you* did. Does this mean we're breaking up?"

Oh, good grief, thought Annette. She began to form the body of a horse on the work table in front of her. As she started pulling and shaping the back legs, she considered how she would answer Pete if he brought up the idea of their breaking up.

"I don't know," she'd probably say nervously. "I really only want what's best for everybody."

Then Pete would probably fold his arms and frown. "Wait a minute," he'd say. "It sounds like you don't want to go to the dance with me. Am I right?"

Then she'd get defensive and say, "Everyone can see that you like Penny now, and I know she likes you. After all, I am her best friend."

Then, Annette envisioned Penny overhearing the conversation and stomping over to them, as mad as a hornet. "Annette! What are you doing?" Penny would yell, those flashing green eyes of hers *livid.*

Pete would get angry as well and say, "Annette, I can't believe you're dumping me!"

Annette would be shocked and try to smooth things over by saying, "But Pete, I never meant to hurt you. I just thought … I thought …"

"She loves *Tim!*" Penny would shout so loud that everyone in the sophomore hall would hear it. Annette would become terribly embarrassed, with nowhere to hide.

No, I can't say anything like that, she told herself as the front legs on her horse sculpture began to manifest from the wet clay. But then she started thinking about Tim and how *he* might be feeling right now. She couldn't forget the look on his face last evening at the supper table, and she knew … she just *knew* Tim cared about her, and his feelings had to be crushed because she had asked Pete to the dance instead of him.

She kept remembering Penny's words as well. "Annette,

why *didn't* you?"

Mr. Hendrickson, the Art teacher, disrupted her reverie as he strolled over to study her work in progress. "Nice horse, Annette," he said with a smile.

Annette smiled up at the teacher. "Thanks. At least you guessed right and didn't say it was a dog."

"Keep going on it," urged Mr. Hendrickson as he moved on to the next student.

When the bell rang and it was the break between second and third hours, Annette found Penny at their locker. "Oh hi, Annette," the dark-haired girl said with a smile. "Did you call the sheriff's office?"

"Yes. It took a while," said Annette. Penny offered her a stick of gum from her purse. "A deputy is coming out to my house today after school." Annette accepted the gum and looked around the hallway. "Have you seen Pete?"

"No. Why? Gee, you're awful nervous. Is something wrong?"

"No. Not really." She was relieved when Debbie and Kathy showed up at their locker. Debbie was glowing and excited about going to the Valentines Dance with Terry the next night.

"Are *you* going?" Kathy asked Penny.

"No, are you?"

Kathy covered her mouth and leaned toward them. "I asked Dennis Schaeffer."

"What!" Penny burst out giggling. "You didn't …"

Kathy nodded her head and laughed. "He accepted."

"I thought you didn't like Dennis," said Annette.

Kathy shrugged. "If you remember, he asked me to Homecoming …" She turned to look at Penny. "Before he asked *you*. And since I turned him down, I thought I'd be nice and ask him to the Valentines Dance." She covered her mouth again and looked around to make sure no one could hear. "I still think he's a dunce, but he said he'd go with me. I just wanna go and have some fun."

"I hear we're doubling," Debbie told Annette, her brown eyes sparkling. "Terry said you're going to the dance with Pete Randt."

Annette was aware of Penny's look of interest. She smiled, then nodded. "Yep."

Debbie turned to Penny. "Why didn't you ask someone, Pen?"

"Now who would *I* ask?" Penny replied.

Just then, Annette caught sight of Pete walking down the hall. Penny had seen him too and gave Annette a little shove. "There's Pete. Weren't you looking for him?"

"Uh … yeah." Annette smiled at her friends, then excused herself and started down the hall after the dark-haired farm boy. "Pete!"

He turned around and grinned, then stopped to wait for her. "Annette!"

"Can we talk?" she asked.

"Sure." He waited.

Annette glanced around. "Not here." She led the way toward an area where there were no students hanging around at their lockers.

"This must be serious," said Pete. He smiled down at her and she could feel her heart beating in her chest. She knew she had to get it over with. "Pete, I've been thinking …"

Footsteps behind them interrupted her. Annette glanced over her shoulder and saw Tim Duncan walking down the hall with Susan Reed, the blonde junior girl she'd seen with Janet that day she had overheard them talking about him. Susan was swinging Tim's hand in hers and flirting openly with him. She saw Tim gaze into her face and laugh as they passed by.

Annette's nerve left her. She felt a flush over her face and, for a moment, she couldn't speak. She turned back to Pete and tried to smile at him, but she felt like crying.

"Yeah, what's on your mind?" Pete prompted. He folded his arms, just as she had imagined he would when she had planned what she was going to say to him.

"Uh … I …" Annette had to swallow. She blinked her eyes, then patted Pete's hand and smiled at him. This time it was convincing. "Pete … I'm looking forward to tomorrow night."

Pete chuckled. "Well, I am too. Yes, I sure am …" Pete's eyes followed Tim and Susan down the hall, and Annette was suddenly embarrassed.

"Well, I'd better get my books for English." She turned and headed back to her locker, where Penny, Kathy and Debbie were still chatting.

"Everything okay?" Penny asked her as she retrieved her English book from the locker.

"Everything's groovy," said Annette.

16

Ruby's Appointment

That afternoon in Geometry class, the school secretary came to the classroom with a note to give to Annette. Mr. Raymond continued his lesson after a short pause, and Annette was aware of Pete's eyes on her as she opened the slip of paper and read it. The note was a phone message from her mother.

"Your mother said she will pick you up at the school parking lot at 3:45. She wants you to go with her to an appointment at the health clinic for Ruby."

Somewhat puzzled, Annette folded up the note and dropped it into her purse. She caught Pete's questioning look and smiled to reassure him, then pretended to focus on the blackboard. She wasn't listening to Mr. Raymond's lecture, however. She was wondering why they were taking Ruby to the clinic. Had something happened to Ruby? It didn't sound like an emergency at least, but Mrs. Vetter wanted Annette to be there too. Then she wondered if Terry had also received a note from the office.

When the final bell rang, Annette gathered up her things and stood up to leave. Just then, Pete came to her desk.

"Is something wrong?" He was quite concerned.

"I don't think so," Annette told him as they left the math room together. She quickly explained about her mom picking her up and their taking Ruby to the clinic.

"I hope she's not sick," said Pete.

"Me too."

"Well, I'll see you tomorrow then."

"Okay, Pete." As he disappeared into the crowd, Annette found Penny already at their locker. She explained about her mom's note.

"Gosh, it must be important," said Penny.

"I'll call you tonight," Annette promised. She grabbed her coat and the books she'd need, then hurried toward the exit.

Terry caught up with her just outside. "You must have gotten Mom's note too," he said.

"What's it all about?" asked Annette.

Terry searched the parking lot, then said, "There's Mom now. Come on." He led the way to the Vetters' sedan as it rolled up to the curb. They could see Ruby sitting in the back seat. Mrs. Vetter greeted them as they climbed in, Terry in the front and Annette beside her sister in the back.

Mrs. Vetter explained as she drove to the clinic next to Ravensville's hospital. "I made an appointment for Ruby to see Doctor Randall, a psychiatrist."

"She's going to talk to me about my dreams," Ruby interjected with a grin.

Annette nodded in understanding.

When they arrived at the clinic, Mrs. Vetter checked Ruby in while Annette and Terry took seats in the waiting room. Annette had just started to page through a teen magazine when a door opened and somebody came out into the waiting area. Annette looked up and recognized the large woman with glasses and long braided gray hair as Lucy Pruett, Fred's wife, from the horse farm.

Mrs. Pruett immediately recognized Annette and walked

over to her, smiling.

"We'll see you next Thursday, Mrs. Pruett," the nurse called after her.

"I'm surprised to see you here, Annette," the woman said. "Are you a patient of Doctor Randall?"

Annette exchanged glances with Terry, then said, "Oh no, we're just here with our sister."

Lucy Pruett turned and saw Ruby at the desk with Mrs. Vetter. "Oh, I see."

Annette was dying of curiosity to know why Fred Pruett's wife was seeing a psychiatrist, but she was too polite to ask. She remembered how frantic the woman had been when they had been in the horse barn that day with Fred and Uncle Will. It began to make sense that perhaps Lucy had some kind of a mental or emotional problem. She recalled how easily she had gone into hysterics over the disturbance in her chicken house.

The nurse came over and handed Lucy a slip of paper. "Don't forget your prescription, Lucy. Remember to call Doctor Randall if you have any more episodes."

Mrs. Pruett thrust the paper into her purse and smiled at all of them, then went out the door. Mrs. Vetter and Ruby took seats across from Annette and Terry.

"Oh, was that the lady at the horse farm?" Ruby asked Annette. "I thought I had seen her before."

"Yes," said Annette. She was explaining the situation to Terry when the nurse came out and called to Ruby.

"Want us to come in?" Terry asked.

Mrs. Vetter shook her head. "Not yet." She followed Ruby into the doctor's office and the nurse closed the door behind them.

While they waited, Terry chatted with Annette. "I'll bet you're excited about tomorrow night," he said with a smile.

Annette hoped her reply was convincing. "Oh, sure. Are you?"

Terry studied her face. "Why did it take you so long to ask Pete to the dance?"

Annette's face reddened. "Uh … I had other things on my mind, such as …" She thought of something quickly. "Such as the livestock rustlers and … and … Ruby's nightmares."

"I hope those scoundrels are caught soon," said Terry.

Annette explained how she'd reported the medallion to the sheriff's department and was waiting for them to follow up on the lead. "My guess is that they are locals."

"Well, it certainly sounds like it," agreed Terry. "I mean, how else would they know who had livestock and where to find them?"

"I can't believe they are getting away with this," added Annette.

They had both returned to reading their magazines when the door opened again and the nurse summoned Annette and Terry into the inner office, where Ruby and Mrs. Vetter sat across the desk of a red-haired woman in her fifties, whose hair was coifed and she wore emerald earrings and a matching green necklace.

"Thanks for waiting outside while I talked to your mother and Ruby," the doctor told them as the nurse directed them into the two remaining seats. "I'm Doctor Randall."

Annette and Terry introduced themselves.

"Ruby has told me about her unfortunate experiences in Colorado." The doctor folded her hands on top of the desk. "The trauma she suffered is no doubt causing her unpleasant dreams as her mind tries to work through the disturbing memories. I understand that you two are very close to Ruby and want what's best for her. Am I right?"

Both Annette and Terry nodded, and the doctor went on.

"Ruby is going to relate any dreams or memories she might have in the future to either of you, so that it will help her clarify the events in order for her to resolve the issues she needs to face, in order to heal from the tremendous stress she is under. Are you, Terry and Annette, willing to hear Ruby's dreams and, if necessary, make notes of what she might say, in case it might assist us all?"

"Sure," said Terry.

"If you think it will help," Annette added.

Mrs. Vetter went over a page the doctor handed her and they decided on an appointment schedule for Ruby to have one-on-one sessions. Then they all left the clinic and headed home.

"Please don't tell anyone I'm seeing a shrink," Ruby begged as they drove out of the downtown area.

"We won't," Annette assured her.

"Ruby, it's really nothing to be ashamed of," said Mrs. Vetter.

"But nobody outside the family needs to know," said Terry.

"Of course, Uncle Will can know," said Ruby. "He's family too."

When they got home, the sun was starting to go down. Ginger greeted them joyfully and Annette changed out of her school clothes and headed right to the barn to do the milking. Now that she was alone, her mind began to dwell on what laid heavily on her heart. She had almost broken off her Valentines Dance date with Pete this morning, but then she had seen Susan Reed with Tim.

Susan Reed, the tall, curvy blonde who had first asked Terry to the dance and been turned down by her brother, was now making a play for Tim. Annette was crushed. Yet she still wondered if *she* had asked Tim, would be have accepted her invitation? She wondered if he was going to the dance with Susan. It began to gnaw on her, and she dreaded the very thought of it.

After supper that night, Mrs. Vetter helped Ruby bake sugar cookies for Valentines Day. Terry was in the living room watching TV and Annette declined to help with the cookies and gave the excuse that she had to do her homework. While she was upstairs sulking, the phone rang and Mrs. Vetter called up the stairway to her. "It's Penny. She wants to talk to you."

Annette closed her French book and went downstairs to the dining room. Ruby was using the heart-shaped cookie cutter and stamping the dough. Annette picked up the phone. "Hi, Pen," she said.

"Oh, Annette, you'll never guess!" squealed Penny at the other end.

Annette sighed. She already knew that Penny was going to tell her that Tim was going to the dance with Susan.

"Annette, I asked Steve Newton to the Valentines Dance," Penny continued excitedly. "And never in a million years did I expect him to say yes."

"What!" cried Annette. "Penny! You mean, he actually is going with you?"

Penny squealed again. "Can you believe it? I just about fell over."

"Penny, that's amazing!" Annette laughed. "Steve Newton! The guy you've been head over heels with for all these years."

"Well …" Penny lowered her voice. "Let's just say it's nothing short of a miracle. After all, everyone always thought he was too stuck up to ask anyone out."

"But you asked *him*."

"Precisely." Penny giggled. "I can't believe it."

"Well, how are you gonna get to the dance? Are you meeting him at the school?"

"Oh no," said Penny. "Tim's taking me. Oh yeah … today Susan Reed asked Tim to the dance. So he's going with her, and he said I could ride along and he'll even pick Steve up at his house."

Annette's heart sank and she couldn't speak. What she had feared had happened.

"Annette … are you there?" Penny asked after a moment of silence.

Annette sighed. "Yeah, Pen."

"What's wrong?"

"N-nothing."

"Everything okay? Is Ruby okay? Pete told me on the bus about her appointment."

Annette knew her mom and Ruby could hear, so she didn't want to disclose too much information, since Ruby didn't want people to know about everything she was dealing with. "Oh, Ruby's fine," she said. "It was nothing. Pen, I'm so happy for you. I hope you have a good time at the dance with Steve."

"Well, what about you?" asked Penny. "I hope you have a great time with Pete."

There was another silence, and then in the background Annette could hear Mrs. Duncan calling to Penny. "I've got to get back to my homework," said Annette. "See you tomorrow."

After she hung up, Annette was relieved that Mrs. Vetter and Ruby were involved in the cookie making because her eyes had already started to well up as she ran back upstairs to her room and closed the door, so no one could hear her cry.

17

Valentine Cookies

It was late when the phone rang again at the Vetters' farmhouse. Annette had gotten into her nightgown and was brushing her teeth when Terry called to her from the stairs. "Annette, Deputy Forni is on the phone. She wants to talk to you."

Not quite done, Annette quickly rinsed her mouth out and wiped her chin with a wash cloth, then hurried downstairs.

"Hello," she said when she picked up the telephone.

"Miss Vetter?" The woman deputy had a slightly husky voice.

"Yes, this is Annette."

"I'm Deputy Forni from the Jackson County Sheriff's Office. We wanted to let you know that the information you provided us with this morning has led us to a young man who lives outside Black River Falls. His name is Bruce Lupenski and he is the owner of the county fair medallion you found on your property."

"Oh," said Annette.

The deputy continued. "We are wondering if you know Bruce."

"No, I've never heard of him," said Annette.

"Well," said Deputy Forni, "Bruce Lupenski claims he is a friend of your family and was visiting you last evening. He says he must have dropped the medallion in your yard."

"But we don't know him," Annette protested. Terry was hovering near the phone and she turned to him. "Terry, do you know a Bruce Lupenski?"

Terry shook his head and shrugged.

"Miss Vetter, are you sure no one in your family is acquainted with this young man?"

"Quite sure," Annette replied. "I saw someone running past our chicken house in the dark when I came out of the barn. I was the only one home and my dog was barking and chased after him." She then explained how she had heard a truck engine start up and had seen vehicle lights as somebody left in a hurry down the road.

"Thank you, Miss Vetter," said the deputy.

"Are you going to arrest him?" asked Annette.

The deputy sighed. "We don't have enough evidence to do that," she admitted. "But since his story about the medallion does not appear to be accurate, I'm going to recommend an investigation."

Annette sighed in defeat. "Yeah, I guess that's all you can do right now." Then she asked if any more livestock had disappeared. The deputy said there had been no more reports of activity because of the rustlers.

"What about any more clues?" asked Annette. "No witnesses at all?"

"No. Well …" The deputy paused, then said, "except Mrs. Pruett at the Pruett horse farm. She might have seen something, but she's not a reliable witness at this point."

"Why not?" Annette asked boldly. She remembered seeing Lucy Pruett in Doctor Randall's office that afternoon, getting a prescription.

"I can't discuss the case. Sorry, Annette. But I will be sure to let you know the minute we apprehend whoever is committing these crimes." With that, the deputy courteously ended the call and Annette hung up the phone.

Terry wanted to know the details and Annette repeated them as Ruby wandered into the kitchen, dressed in her red-and-white polka dot pajamas.

"My valentines cookies are ready to take to school tomorrow," the younger girl said with sparkling blue eyes and a smile.

"And they sure smell good." Annette smiled back at her sister.

"You can taste one," prompted Ruby.

"No, I just brushed my teeth," Annette groaned.

"Well, *I'll* have one." Terry reached for one of the heart-shaped cookies with pink frosting that had been set aside on a platter for the family to eat. He took a bite, then said, "Mmmm."

Annette stuck her head into the living room, where Mrs. Vetter was knitting and watching a show on television. "Good night, Mom."

"See you in the morning, dear," replied Mrs. Vetter.

Annette followed Ruby upstairs to their bedroom and climbed into her side of the bed to read for a few minutes before lights-out. The younger girl snuggled beneath the covers and went to sleep almost instantly. Annette was often amazed how easily Ruby could fall asleep.

She ended up reading longer than usual. She heard Terry go to his room next door to the girls, and a few minutes later Mrs. Vetter turned off the hall light and shut her bedroom door at the other end of the hallway.

Annette's mind was still on Tim and the sad fact that he was going to the Valentines Dance with Susan Reed instead of herself. Of course, she realized that Penny's brother had always been a lady's man at Ravensville High. Most the girls in the school were attracted to him because of his good looks and his magnetic personality. The fact that he paid extra attention to *her* had always made Annette feel she was special to him.

Even though she had come to like Pete, and had certainly been bedazzled by his college-age cousin last October, Annette had harbored deep feelings for Tim from a very young age. She knew they had a rapport, yet she felt too insecure and afraid to follow her heart's desire.

Annette couldn't concentrate any longer on her book, so she placed the bookmark inside, then set the book on her bedside table and reached over to turn off the lamp.

In the darkness of the room, she stared up at the ceiling and listened to Ruby's breathing. She regretted writing the words on Tim's birthday card. Not because they weren't true words. She had meant every word. But had it been too bold of her to express such personal feelings? Had she only managed to push Tim away when a simple "Happy Birthday from Annette" would have been adequate?

Oh dear, Annette thought as she rolled onto her side and pulled the covers over her ears. She then tried to recall the exact words she had written so carefully on the inside of the card. She had thought hard about what to write and had almost chickened out.

Dear Tim, she had written, *You are such a wonderful person to have in my life. I have known you since I can remember, and even though you would tease me a lot, I cherished you more than a friend.*

Then she had added, *I hope we can have some good times ahead before you leave for college. Affectionately, Annette.*

She had hesitated to write the words from her heart, but at the last moment, when she had hurried up to her bedroom to get his card before she and Terry met Penny to walk to the bus stop, she had quickly penned the memorized words and then sealed the envelope.

Now she realized that perhaps it had been a mistake. *Girls are not supposed to be forward,* she told herself. She had crossed the line, ruined any chances she might have had to become Tim's steady girlfriend. Annette sniffed as a tear pushed its way onto her pillow. What a fool she had been.

Annette slowly sat up in bed, then got up to head to the bathroom, where she could cry a little and blow her nose without disturbing Ruby. Ginger heard her and got up, shaking his collar.

Then, before Annette could reach the bedroom door, Ruby started thrashing around in bed, moaning and gasping. Another bad dream! Annette stood still and waited to see if it would pass. For a few seconds, she thought Ruby had settled back into a peaceful slumber, but then the girl began whimpering and her breathing grew labored.

Annette went to her side and gently grabbed her shoulders. "Ruby … Ruby, wake up."

Her sister sobbed as she came out of the dream. "Annette … *oh no* … he needs help!"

Annette walked over to turn on the bedside lamp, then sat in bed as Ruby rubbed her eyes. She was shaking. "Tell me your dream. What happened?" she asked.

"It-it-it wasn't about me," Ruby stammered. She broke down and covered her face with her hands, then sobbed and looked up at Annette's face, her blue eyes red and expanded. "It was … it was … my *dad*. Oh, Annette, he is going to *die* … I'm so afraid for him …" She sobbed some more.

Annette took the girl into her arms and comforted her. "Ruby, it was only a dream."

"No. No, it was more than a dream," Ruby insisted. "It was so *real*."

"Okay," said Annette. "Doctor Randall said you should

tell me or Terry everything that's in your dreams, so that it will help you remember. Do you think you can do that?"

Ruby finally got hold of herself, relaxed by Annette's closeness and the softness of her voice. "Yes. I'll tell you." She sniffed and reached for a tissue. "He was in a jungle. I think it was Vietnam."

"Go on," said Annette.

Ruby sighed. "It was very hot there, with all kinds of nasty flies and bugs everywhere. There was mud and rain … and-and … my dad was really sick."

"What else?"

Ruby continued. "There was someone with him. I don't know … but my dad was struggling to walk. He could barely stand up. The other man in my dream was making him keep moving. He was shouting at him, telling him he had to keep going or they would be killed." She looked at Annette, then said, "And that's all. You woke me up. I don't know if he made it … or-or … *not.*" Ruby wailed.

"Shhh." Annette held Ruby tight and rocked her. "It's going to be all right," she said. But she didn't understand this dream. Most of Ruby's nightmares had to do with the abuse she had experienced at the foster home in Colorado. And now she was having dreams about her military dad in Vietnam, who was thought to be dead.

Fortunately, Terry and Mrs. Vetter had not been awakened by Ruby's nightmare this time. Annette managed to get Ruby settled down again after they changed the subject and talked about all the fun they would have when the weather warmed up.

Then it helped a lot when Clyde, Ruby's gray tabby kitten, came into their room and jumped up on the bed. The blonde girl cradled the cat in her arms and Clyde purred contentedly beside Ruby's head as she lay back down. Soon Annette was able to turn off the light and was now so exhausted emotionally, she slipped right off to sleep.

Friday morning came too soon for Annette. She awoke to Ginger gently nudging her shoulder as daylight started coming through the bedroom window. Ruby slept peacefully. Clyde had left sometime during the night. Annette quietly got up, grabbed her clothes, and went to the bathroom to dress before going out to milk the cows and do her chores.

When she came inside for breakfast, everyone was up. Mrs. Vetter had made coffee, and Terry was sitting at the kitchen table beside Ruby, enjoying scrambled eggs and bacon. Ginger went to his feed dish, which Ruby had promptly filled with his kibble.

"Happy Valentines Day!" Ruby grinned as she picked up her glass of orange juice.

"Oh ... Happy Valentines to you, too," Annette replied with a smile.

"You look tired, Annette," said Mrs. Vetter. "Are you feeling all right?"

"I'm fine," said Annette as she took her place at the table with a cup of coffee. Terry pushed the creamer her way, and she reached for the sugar bowl.

"It's my fault," admitted Ruby. "I had a bad dream again."

Mrs. Vetter and Terry turned to her with interest.

"I told Annette about it," Ruby disclosed.

"No wonder you're tired," said Terry.

"It was about Dad," Ruby said, growing suddenly sullen.

"Well, I'm sorry about that," said Mrs. Vetter.

Terry looked at his sister. "It wasn't about Colorado Springs?"

"Not this time," said Ruby. "But I've already told Annette, so I don't want to think about it."

"You don't have to," assured Mrs. Vetter. "After all, it is

Valentines Day."

Ruby brightened. "Maybe Uncle Will is coming this weekend."

"Now, actually, it was supposed to be a surprise," said Mrs. Vetter, "but Uncle Will *is* going to be here tonight. He called me yesterday to say he was thinking about driving up."

"Hurray!" Ruby cheered, then took a bite out of her toast.

Later, as Annette and Terry joined Penny on their walk to the bus stop, Annette told them what Ruby's dream had been about. Terry was somber, but Penny, as usual, had something to say about it.

"Gosh, Annette, maybe Ruby is actually having telepathy with her dad."

"Telepathy?" Terry scrunched up his face. "You mean … mind-reading?"

Annette smirked. "Penny's into the supernatural again."

"Well, why not?" cried Penny. "I've done a lot of reading on the subject … and on dreams."

"Maybe you should go to school to become a psychiatrist," said Terry, and Annette gave him a warning look, afraid he might let it slip about Ruby's visits with the shrink.

"Not a psychiatrist," said Penny. "A parapsychologist. Yes, that's what I might like to be." She smiled to herself. "It's just so fascinating to read about all that stuff. You know, ghosts … psychic phenomena … even UFOs."

"UFOs?" scoffed Terry.

Annette shot him a warning look, and then decided to change the subject. "Well, tonight's the big night … the Valentines Dance … and all three of us are going."

"And Tim," Penny had to add.

Terry looked startled. "Tim's going? Who asked him?"

"Susan Reed," said Penny.

"Oh." Terry made a face.

"That's right," said Penny, "she asked *you* first, didn't

she?"

"Why didn't you go to the dance with Susan?" Annette asked her brother.

Terry shrugged. "No reason."

"Come on, Terry, spill it. What's wrong with Susan?" asked Penny.

"Nothing's *wrong* with her," said Terry. "I just didn't decide on the spot. Then Debbie asked me." He smiled, obviously embarrassed.

"Susan's really pretty," said Penny, "but she's not exactly Tim's type."

Annette didn't want to discuss Tim nor Susan right now. But Penny wouldn't leave it alone.

"Actually, Tim hasn't been dating anyone for weeks."

"I'm still in shock that Steve Newton is going to the dance with you," Annette said, to try and change the subject.

Penny rolled her eyes. "Yeah … well …"

"But I'm glad you're gonna be there," said Annette. "It'll be *fun*." She hoped that her tone was convincing, but she had the feeling that both her brother and her best friend could see that she was trying too hard to cover up her true feelings.

For two days now, Joe had followed Lloyd Lovingood and the two Vietnamese guides through the jungle. The heat was unbearable and the sweat on his body drew flies and mosquitoes as they moved stealthily through the thickest areas, always on the lookout for anyone who might cause them harm.

Joe remembered all too well the torture and the threat of death he had faced in the hands of the Viet Cong. More of his memories were coming back to him during the difficult trek since leaving Kim-Ly's village. He had no idea where they were headed, or where they were, even … but he had no choice but to trust Mr. Lovingood and the men he had entrusted with their lives.

They rarely spoke to one another. It was vital to remain as quiet and hidden as they possibly could. At night they would camp in areas that the guides had scouted out and declared safe. But now Joe was at the mercy of polluted water and questionable rations. He was strong enough to go without food, but the exertion and the tremendous heat and humidity forced him to drink water from the streams or swamps. He just hoped his immune system could cope after all he had been through.

18

A Trip to the Horse Farm

"Looks like you have company," Penny said that afternoon as she and Annette saw the familiar yellow station wagon parked in the driveway behind Mrs. Vetter's car. Terry had ridden home with Tim to put in a couple of hours work at the Duncan farm.

"Uncle Will's here," Annette revealed. "Mom said he was coming today."

"Then I guess I'll see you tonight at the dance," Penny told her as they parted at the end of the driveway.

"Okay," said Annette. "See you there." She hurried up the gravel path that was spotted with crusty patches of snow. Dried brown grass stuck up through the sunny areas of the lawn. She was glad her school day had passed fairly quickly, for once. She wasn't expecting the dance to be anything memorable and she actually dreaded having to watch Tim dancing with Susan.

"Annette's home!" called Ruby when Annette stepped through the back door. Ginger trotted over to greet her, his tail swishing. She could hear the adults' voices talking and laughing from the living room as she hung up her coat. Ruby still had her school dress on and was grinning with excitement.

"Were your valentine cookies a hit at school?" Annette asked her sister.

"Yes!" Ruby spun around in a circle. "Come in here!" She beckoned Annette to the living room.

"Hello, Annette," Uncle Will called to her from his favorite chair in the corner. Mrs. Vetter was seated on the couch with her legs crossed. On the coffee table in front of her was a huge vase full of a dozen red roses.

"Wow!" cried Annette. "Look at those!"

"Uncle Will brought them for Mom," said Ruby, who bent over the bouquet to sniff them.

"They're beautiful," said Annette. She noticed Uncle Will's pleased expression, and she glanced at her mother to see that Mrs. Vetter didn't seem at all disturbed that he had brought her flowers. She wondered what this really meant.

"Aren't they?" Mrs. Vetter stood up and smiled. "Well, I'd better get started on the meat loaf."

"Happy Valentines Day, Uncle Will," said Annette.

"Same to you," he said.

Clyde, who had been grooming herself on top of the television set, suddenly jumped down and ran across the room to pounce on one of her mouse toys. Ruby laughed and sat down to play with her kitten. Ginger walked over to Uncle Will and sat down as the man stroked the collie's white mane.

The phone rang in the dining room. Since Mrs. Vetter was in there to answer it, Annette sat down on the sofa across from Uncle Will and watched Ruby play with her kitten. "I'm glad you could come up this weekend," she said.

"Oh! I almost forgot." Ruby jumped up from the floor and ran to the bookshelf to get some pink envelopes. She gave one to Uncle Will, then handed Annette the other one. She had written their names in swirly letters. "Your valentines! I made them myself."

"Thank you, Ruby," said Annette.

Just then, Mrs. Vetter stood in the doorway to the living room. "Will, Fred Pruett's on the phone for you."

Uncle Will carried his valentine with him to the dining room while Annette slowly opened hers. Ruby watched with a smile as Annette opened the card, which Ruby had crafted with cut-out hearts, glitter and magazine pictures. Annette's card had a Holstein cow on the front and a message that read, "To Annette. I'm so glad you are my big sister. I love you. Ruby."

"Oh, it's great ... thanks, Ruby." Annette stood up to give her sister a hug.

Uncle Will came back into the living room. "I have to drive over to the Pruett farm. Annette, would you like to come along?"

Surprised, Annette set her card down on the coffee table as Ruby laughed and went back to playing with the cat. She looked up at Uncle Will and said, "Well, sure ... I'll ride along."

"Ruby?" Uncle Will asked.

"I think I'll stay here with Clyde," Ruby said.

Annette followed Uncle Will to the kitchen, where Mrs. Vetter was starting dinner. He quickly explained that he needed to make a run over to the horse farm and wanted Annette to come along. Mrs. Vetter nodded her head at them in consent.

In the station wagon as they drove toward town, Annette waited for an explanation, but Uncle Will was quiet and obviously had something weighing on his mind. Finally, she had to ask. "Uncle Will, why do you need to go see Mr. Pruett right now?"

"Fred asked me to come," said Uncle Will, "and I wanted to show you something."

"Can you tell me what it is?" asked Annette.

"I think you'll understand when you see for yourself." Uncle Will glanced at her with a quick smile, then drove in silence. Annette watched out the window as they cruised through downtown Ravensville, then turned east onto the county road that went out past the Kowalski farm.

When they arrived at the Pruett horse farm, a beat-up white pickup was parked alongside the other vehicles the Pruetts owned. Uncle Will parked the station wagon, and as they got out Fred Pruett walked toward them from the front porch, dressed in his sheepskin jacket.

"Hello, Will," he called. He nodded at Annette. "Nice to see you too, young lady."

"Let's head over to the barn," Fred said with a glance over his shoulder. Annette looked toward the front of the house and wondered why Mr. Pruett appeared a little nervous. She presumed Lucy was inside the house as she followed the two men toward the barn.

With the sun starting to settle in the west, she hoped they wouldn't be staying too long. She still had to milk the cows and get ready for the dance. Again, she questioned why it had been so important for her to come to the farm with Uncle Will.

In the barn, Fred and Uncle Will exchanged some banter as they led their way to the stall at the very end, where Sundown was munching some grain from a manger. Annette looked around and noticed some empty stalls as well.

"I thought you might like to see how the mare is doing," Fred Pruett said to Annette. "Your uncle and I have been talking about negotiating a price on her colt."

Annette's mouth dropped open. "What?" She looked at Uncle Will.

"Well, it's all going to depend, of course, on what Fred wants to charge after Sundown's given birth."

"But you'll be the first one to get a chance to buy her colt," Fred added with a smile.

"Wow …" Annette breathed, and leaned over the railing of the stall to watch the mother of her future horse. She was starting to believe that maybe it was really going to happen … she and Penny were going to get their horse … with Uncle Will's help, perhaps.

They heard a noise in the front of the barn, and turned to see a teen-aged boy who had just entered the barn. He was about 18 years old, Annette guessed, with a cowboy hat, a denim jacket and blue jeans, with curly reddish-brown hair.

"Come on in, B.J.," called Fred. "Will, Annette … this is Lucy's nephew, B.J."

The boy came over, but he didn't smile. He kept staring at Annette.

"B.J., this is my old friend, Will Knutson, and his niece, Annette."

B.J. thrust his hand out, and Annette shook it, then Will followed suit.

"Are you visiting?" Will asked the boy.

B.J. appeared apprehensive as he stared from Uncle Will to Fred, then Annette and back to Uncle Will. "Naw," he said. "Aunt Lucy needed some help fixin' up the chicken house. She's gettin' a new order of chicks in a week or two. She wants to be ready for 'em."

"Well, Annette here has chickens," said Uncle Will.

B.J. didn't appear impressed at all. Annette noticed that as he stuck his hands in his pockets and looked around, he seemed to carry some resentment toward Fred.

"Do you live around here?" Annette asked him.

"He lives outside Black River Falls," Fred explained. "B.J., I wanted you to meet Annette because *she's* probably going to buy Sundown's colt next summer."

Annette noticed that Fred put heavy emphasis on the fact that she might be buying his colt, and she wondered why.

B.J. looked startled when Fred said that and his eyes expanded with recognition as he glared at Annette. "*You?*"

Annette blushed and Uncle Will nodded his head at her.

She wondered what Uncle Will knew that he wasn't telling her about the boy.

Suddenly, B.J. turned and headed out the barn.

"Where you going, boy?" called Fred. "Come back here."

B.J. stopped and sighed impatiently, staring at the floor.

"Annette … B.J. said he knew you," Fred continued.

Annette's mouth dropped open. "I don't …" Then she stopped. Black River Falls had been mentioned and she recalled the conversation on the phone last night with Deputy Forni. Then she made the connection. *B.J.!* She asked him, "Is your first name Bruce? Bruce Lupenski?"

The boy continued to stare at his feet, then frowned. "Yeah," he finally admitted.

"The one who dropped the medallion from the county fair on our property?"

At once B.J. grew defensive. "It isn't what you think."

"But why did you tell the sheriff you were visiting me? Just what were you doing on our property?" Annette demanded.

Bruce had fire in his eyes. "Nothing," he said. "I didn't *do* anything."

"But were you outside our barn two nights ago?"

"I lost the medallion a long time ago," Bruce stated.

"So you didn't drop it?"

"No," he retorted.

"Well, why did you tell them you knew me?"

"I don't know!" he shouted.

"Then you have no idea who might have been snooping around the Vetter farm?" asked Fred. His voice had turned hard.

"That's right," said the boy. Then he started walking out of the barn. He turned and said, "Aunt Lucy said supper's on in twenty minutes." Then he hurried away.

"And … I'd better get this young lady home," Uncle Will said to Fred. "She's got a date tonight."

Fred rubbed his chin and looked Annette over. "Is that right?"

"It's the Valentines Dance," Annette explained nervously.

"Look, I apologize for B.J.'s manner," said Fred as they started to leave the barn. "He's had a rough childhood and Lucy's always stuck up for him … treated him better than his own mother."

When they reached the driveway, Uncle Will reached out and shook the other man's hand, and said, "Thanks, Fred."

Annette was glad to get back into the yellow station wagon. Uncle Will started up the engine.

"What was *that* all about?" Annette finally asked Uncle Will after they got on their way.

"I wanted you to know that if you decide you and Penny want that colt, I'll be happy to help finance the deal," Uncle Will told her as he drove.

Annette smiled. "Oh, Uncle Will, that's so kind of you. But … but …"

"*And* … I wanted that boy to know who you are." He looked at Annette, then explained. "Fred has been kind of concerned about his wife. Lucy has a mild disorder known as manic-depression. She gets a little out of control at times. Anyway, that's beside the point. The sheriff's deputy came out and talked to Lucy and Fred about Bruce … B.J., they call him. Apparently your name was mentioned in reference to the medallion you found with the kid's name on it. So Fred called me up last night and told me about it, and we wanted to see what reaction he'd have … if he really knew you or not."

"I wonder why he lied about it," said Annette.

"Well, if he didn't lose the medallion on your property, the question is … who did?"

Annette pondered the mystery while they drove home. The sky had grown rosy and dusk was settling in by the time Uncle Will pulled into the Vetter's driveway.

Inside the house, the meat loaf aroma filled the kitchen. Annette had not changed out of her school dress yet, so had to go upstairs and change before going to the barn.

When she came downstairs, Ruby and Mrs. Vetter came in from outside. "We did the milking for you, Annette," Ruby said with a grin. "I milked Elizabeth *all by myself.*"

Mrs. Vetter winked at Annette as she hung up her coat. "Ruby's learning fast."

"*You* milked the cow?" asked Uncle Will.

"Thank you, Mom." Annette gave her mother a hug.

"I know you want to get ready for the dance," said Mrs. Vetter.

Annette glanced up at the clock. "Where's Terry?"

"He just got out of the shower," said Ruby.

"Supper will be ready in fifteen minutes," said Mrs. Vetter.

"I think I have time to set my hair." Annette ran up the stairs and tried to dismiss the strange encounter with Bruce Lupenski as she concentrated on the night ahead of her.

19

The Valentines Dance

There hadn't been time to shampoo her hair first, so Annette did the best she could with her rollers before joining the rest of the family for supper.

Mrs. Vetter's meat loaf was outstanding, but Annette's appetite had diminished, along with her enthusiasm for the night ahead. She picked at the food on her plate while her mother and Uncle Will conversed about past events. Mrs. Vetter was bringing up Annette's and Terry's father quite a bit, she noticed.

"I remember Tom's and my first Valentines Day," Mrs. Vetter said with a dreamy smile and a distant gaze into thin air. "He showed up at my dorm room in Eau Claire with a box of chocolates and three long-stemmed roses."

"*Only* three?" teased Ruby as she spooned some apple-sauce onto her plate.

Mrs. Vetter sighed. "Yes … three," she said. "And when I asked him why he'd brought me three red roses, Tom said, 'That's how many children you're going to have.' And then he planted a kiss on my cheek."

Annette glanced over at Uncle Will, who was busy eating a second helping of the meat loaf. He asked Terry to pass him the ketchup.

Ruby giggled. "Well, he was right, you know."

"Yeah, Mom," said Terry as he handed the ketchup bottle to his uncle. "You do have three children now."

Annette looked at her mother and smiled. "That's right, Mom. You've got me, Terry and Ruby."

"We'd better get ready to go," Terry said to Annette. He wiped his mouth with a napkin, then stood up. "I told Debbie we'd pick her up at seven-fifteen."

"I'll run upstairs and get ready." Annette pushed back her chair and took her half-empty plate to the sink. Then she climbed the stairs, starting to remove the rollers from her head as she went to her room to brush out her set. Then she selected the dress she had decided to wear, a red and white one with an empire waist and three-quarter length sleeves. It had a small V neck that would look nice with her heart locket. She opened her dresser drawer to get it out of the jewelry box, then put on the necklace with the gold chain before changing clothes.

"Groovy dress, Annette!" exclaimed Ruby when Annette came down the stairs in her red outfit, wearing her black Sunday shoes with just a slight heel. At least her nylons didn't have any runs started.

Annette smiled and gave her sister a hug.

"Ready?" Terry emerged from the dining room, already dressed in his long black coat, his blond hair combed neatly off to one side.

"Yes." Annette went to put on her coat and Mrs. Vetter peeked in from the dining room.

"Have a good time," said her mother. "Terry, drive carefully."

"I will," he promised.

Annette felt the chill of the winter night air as she climbed into the passenger seat. Terry started the engine and waited a minute for it to warm up, then drove toward the Randt farm on Gaston Road.

"When are you gonna learn to drive?" Terry asked on the way.

"I dunno," said Annette. "Soon, I'm sure. Mom's been busy."

"Has Penny started driving?"

"Not unless Tim took her out. She hasn't said anything about it."

"Well, the weather will be warming up soon," said Terry. "I think you should start learning."

Annette sighed. She had dreamed of Tim being the one to teach her how to drive. Now it looked as though that wasn't likely to happen.

When they arrived at the Randts', Terry waited in the driveway and kept the car running while Annette got out and went to the door. The Randt children were excited to see her. The youngest ones were already in their pajamas, and Mr. Randt was rounding them up for bed as Pete came out of the kitchen, dressed in a yellow shirt, green sweater vest and brown dress pants. He grinned when he saw her.

"You look nice," Annette told him.

"Thanks." Pete grabbed his coat and they went out the door and down the porch steps to the waiting car.

"I didn't see your mom," said Annette.

"Oh, she's upstairs with baby Laura."

Annette nodded as the two of them climbed into the back seat. Terry and Pete greeted each other, and then Terry backed out of the long driveway and headed toward Ravensville. The two boys did all the talking on the way. Annette just sat, staring out the car window at the dark fields, feeling depressed.

They arrived at Debbie Kelton's house in town a couple of minutes before seven-fifteen. She didn't wait for Terry to come get her, but flew out the door as soon as the car pulled in.

Debbie wore a big grin on her face as she hurried over to the car. Terry reached across the front seat to open the passenger door for her, and Debbie wiggled in, turning to Annette in the back seat. "This is going to be so much fun!"

Annette couldn't help but admire Debbie's enthusiasm. She, at least, was going to the Valentines Dance with the boy she wanted.

Terry seemed equally happy and now the two up front carried on the conversation as Terry drove to the high school. Annette and Pete sat quietly in the back seat and didn't look at one another.

Annette sighed and stared at couples heading from the parking lot to the school gymnasium, where the dance was being held. She wondered if this was going to be a long night.

On the third day of the journey, Joe was spent. He woke up at dawn that morning, covered with sweat and feverish. When Lloyd Lovingood and the two guides attempted to stand him up, he could barely get to his feet. When they had camped in a safe jungle thicket last evening, Joe had felt he was coming down with something. He couldn't eat. Everything made him nauseous. But most of all, he was plagued with fatigue.

"You've got to walk with us," Lovingood encouraged him. "We are not that far from the river."

One of the guides spoke to Lloyd in Vietnamese. Lovingood responded in their language, and Joe understood not a word, but he could tell the two small men were frightened. He got the feeling they wanted to abandon their mission, but the Englishman would not allow it.

"How … far … is it?" Joe managed to utter.

Lovingood consulted with his guides, then replied, "They say only a few more hours till we get to the river, the Hué … but it is dangerous. Viet Cong could be anywhere."

Joe staggered to his feet, but at once grew dizzy and felt

as if he were going to pass out. He heard Lovingood give an order, and then the two guides each took one of his arms and began to drag him, more or less, through the jungle. When Joe groaned, they scolded him, and he knew he had to continue. If he didn't, he would die for sure. Most of all, he didn't want these brave men to die with him.

Surely there couldn't be anything worse than what he had gone through at the Viet Cong prisoner camp, with the torture, the terrible thirst and the fear that his life might end at the whim of his captors. But Joe felt so bad right now, he began to think that death was the easy way out.

A nnette and Pete followed Terry and Debbie into the gymnasium, where they heard loud rock and roll music coming from speakers set up on the stage. The lights were dimmed and there were red lamps and valentine decorations up on all the walls. Couples were mingling all around them, and a table had been set up with pink crepe paper for a table-cloth, and a large punch bowl full of a red drink.

After they removed their coats on the bleachers, they looked around at the crowd. Pete took Annette's hand and led her over to the refreshment table. She recognized many of her classmates and smiled and greeted them. Both she and Pete were looking the crowd over for familiar faces. A disk jockey was up on the stage, playing records. Only four couples were out on the floor, dancing to a fast tune.

Suddenly Pete said, "There's Penny and Steve. Come on." Without waiting for an answer, he led Annette by the hand over to some chairs that circled the dance floor. Penny had already seen them and her green eyes grew wide as a smile stretched across her face.

"Annette! Pete!" she called.

"Hey, Pete," said Steve Newton, who had put on a light blue sport jacket and tie for the occasion. He had blondish hair and green eyes. His physique and good looks had given him a reputation among the girls at Ravensville High, yet many of Annette's friends had decided he was full of himself. He focused his gaze first on Annette, smiled at her briefly, then diverted his attention back to Pete.

"Your new outfit is lovely," said Annette as she admired Penny's chiffon yellow dress.

"Thanks." Penny grabbed Annette's arm and took her aside. "Isn't this exciting?" But before Annette could answer, Penny pointed across the room. "Oh look, there's Kathy with Dennis Schaeffer." She giggled. "Well, I'm just glad she asked him."

"Me too," said Annette, who was looking over the sea of faces for someone special.

"Debbie and Terry make a cute couple," remarked Penny, glancing in their direction.

"I think so, too," said Annette. "Hey, I want to tell you what happened this afternoon."

"What happened?" asked Penny.

"Uncle Will drove me over to the horse farm."

"The Pruetts'?"

Annette then explained how they had gone into the barn and Fred Pruett had offered to sell Sundown's colt to the girls. "And that's not all," she added. "Uncle Will wants to help us buy it!"

Penny was ecstatic. "Oh, Annette! Wow! Really?"

Then Annette lowered her voice. "And there's something else …" She then explained how the older boy, B.J., had come into the barn, and what had been said about him being Bruce Lupenski, whose medallion she had found near the chicken house.

"Annette! That's real strange …"

"You're telling me," said Annette. "He was acting real nervous. I think Fred set up this meeting so that he could know if Bruce was telling the truth about knowing me … and of course, he didn't."

"Oh, Annette … but you said he denied dropping the medallion. Didn't he say he lost it a few months ago?"

"That's what he said," said Annette, "but I'm not so sure he was telling the truth."

"Gosh," said Penny. "And he's Mrs. Pruett's nephew?"

"Yup." Annette didn't want to bring up the subject of Lucy Pruett's mental disorder, because it might lead to Ruby's visit to the health clinic and she had promised Ruby she wouldn't say anything.

"I think Pete wants you." Penny turned and smiled as the dark-haired boy came over to them, followed by Steve, who was looking around with his hands in his pockets.

"Want some punch, Annette?"

"I'm not that thirsty," she said.

"I'll take some," said Penny.

Pete grinned at her, and the two of them wandered toward the refreshment table. Annette glanced at Steve, who didn't seem in the least worried about his date's whereabouts. He wasn't acting too friendly toward her, so Annette moved through the crowd a little and caught sight of Terry dancing with Debbie out on the floor. She watched them a moment, pleased that her brother seemed happy tonight.

Then, Annette saw Tim across the room. He was standing beside Susan Reed, and apparently they had just arrived at the dance because she was removing her coat. He took it from her and laid it beside his on the bleachers. They exchanged a few words, and then Susan started mingling with some girlfriends she knew.

Tim stood, looking around the gym, and then his eyes locked on Annette's and they stared at one another for several seconds before Annette turned away, embarrassed.

Annette made her way back to the refreshment table,

where Pete and Penny stood together, talking and drinking their punch. She didn't see Steve Newton anywhere and Penny didn't seem bothered by his absence one bit. It was obvious who was the center of her attention.

Annette wandered around the gymnasium and visited with some of her friends. Once in a while she would glance in Tim's direction. Susan had gotten him out on the dance floor already. She saw that Penny was still in conversation with Pete at the punch table, and out on the dance floor, Steve Newton—Penny's *date*—was showing off to a bunch of admiring girls, dancing to a fast song by himself and really hamming it up.

Finally Pete noticed Annette and carried over a glass of fruit punch for her. He smiled apologetically and said, "Sorry, Annette. I didn't mean to ignore you."

Annette accepted the punch and flashed a smile at him. "It's okay, Pete." She noticed Penny searching faces for Steve.

"And … by the way, Happy Valentines Day," said Pete.

"Thank you, Pete."

He stared down at his feet, his hands in his pockets. "Do you … do you wanna dance?"

Annette quickly downed her punch, then set the cup down. "Why not?" She grasped his hand and walked him onto the dance floor just as *Jumpin' Jack Flash* by the Rolling Stones started playing. Soon, most everyone was on the dance floor, hopping and moving around to the contagious music. Pete hesitated at first, but soon caught on and started getting loose.

"Like this?" he shouted.

"Yup, just do what everyone else is doing," Annette yelled back at him. She felt exhilarated by the music, caught up in the mood and the rhythm.

When the number ended, Pete led her to the side, slightly out of breath. "I'm sorry I don't dance very well."

"You did great," Annette encouraged him. A new song had started, another fast dance. She then noticed Steve Newton making a spectacle out of himself on the dance floor. He had three junior girls around him, taking turns with him as he danced from one to the other, coaxing them on.

Penny suddenly appeared out of the crowd and watched Steve's antics. She folded her arms and shook her head slowly.

"Has he danced with you yet?" Annette asked her friend.

Penny shook her head. "I think he forgot I'm his date."

"Oh, that's not right," said Pete. "What's got into him anyway? I mean … why wouldn't Steve Newton want to dance with the prettiest girl in the room?" His smile for Penny was warm and special, and Annette could see the response in Penny's green eyes.

"I'm going to get some more punch," said Annette. "You two … why don't you dance?"

Penny looked momentarily alarmed.

"You ... don't mind?" Pete asked Annette.

She grinned at the two of them. "No, not at all. Go on … get out there and kick up your heels."

Pete took Penny's hand and the two of them went into the midst of the dancers. Penny looked back at Annette helplessly, but Annette only waved her on. She was convinced now that Pete and Penny should have come to the dance together.

"Annette, hi!" Nancy Marshall met her at the refreshment table.

"Nancy, great seeing you," said Annette, looking around. "Who'd you come with?"

Nancy shot a look over her shoulder. "I invited a friend from Darwell Heights. George is a friend of the family." She giggled. "He's not so bad, really."

They chatted awhile, and then Annette decided to visit the restroom to refresh her lipstick. When she came out, she heard the music for a slow, romantic dance playing in the gym. She wandered over to watch the couples on the floor. Pete and Penny were dancing together, their arms draped around each other. She noticed they weren't moving around much, mostly staying in one place.

Then, Annette caught sight of Susan Reed standing next to Terry across the room by the bleachers. Susan was flirting openly with Terry while Debbie was off to the side, talking and laughing with Kathy Evans and Nancy Marshall, who was introducing her friend George to them.

Annette focused on Susan, who was obviously embarrassing Terry, who was trying to be polite, but Annette could see that her brother just wanted to get away from Susan. Debbie finally glanced in their direction and Annette watched as her blonde friend marched over to Terry and beckoned him away from Susan. Terry seemed only too glad to be free from Susan's clutches.

Annette wondered where Tim was. She scanned the sea of faces in the dim gymnasium, but did not see him. When the slow dance ended, Pete and Penny found their way over to her, and Penny said nervously, "You should dance with Pete next."

"No," Annette protested with a smile. "You two just forget about me. Have a good time."

"But …" Pete looked totally confused. "Wait …"

Annette drew a breath, then grabbed each of them and pulled them into a corner where nobody could hear them. "There's something I want to say." Then, before either of them could get a word in, Annette continued, "It's been obvious to me for weeks now, and Pete … the reason it took me so long to get around to inviting you to the dance is because I was waiting for Penny to ask you first."

Penny gave a little squeal and backed up, humiliated.

Pete's baffled expression almost made Annette giggle. "But … but, *Annette*…"

"Penny likes you, Pete," Annette told him. "She didn't want to come between us. She's the best friend anyone could ever have. I've tried to convince her that she should tell you the truth."

Penny started to cry. "Oh, Annette … what are you doing?"

Pete glanced at Penny and asked, "Is it true? Do you … *did* you think about asking me to the dance?"

Then Penny wiped her eyes, recovering her dignity as she spun around to face both of them. "All right. I can't hide it any longer. Annette, I never wanted to steal your boyfriend."

"I know that," Annette said softly. "It makes no difference now. You and Pete are meant for each other."

Pete suddenly gave Annette a quick hug and grinned. "I didn't want to crush your feelings, Annette, but I have to admit … Penny's kinda … *hot*."

Suddenly, both Annette and Penny burst out laughing because of Pete's remark. He joined in. Then, Penny stared up at Pete and blinked, then said to Annette, "So … what does this mean?"

Annette looked into the crowd of people and pointed to Steve Newton, who was now dancing with Susan Reed. "Looks like Steve has deserted you."

"Well, where's Tim?" asked Penny.

"I haven't seen him in a while," said Annette, and Pete just shrugged.

"Well, I don't care," said Penny. "I don't know why I asked that jerk to the dance in the first place."

"I know why," said Annette, and they looked at her questioningly. "You needed to be here tonight. Pete, Penny's your date for the rest of the night."

"Really?" Pete broke into an excited grin. Then he turned to Penny and asked, "Care to dance?"

She laughed and the next thing they knew, Pete and Penny were out on the dance floor again while Annette sighed with relief and slowly wandered over to the bleachers.

She had all kinds of feelings brewing. Relief because she had finally come to terms with her best friend and her boyfriend. Annoyance because of Susan Reed flirting with Terry, then with Steve Newton … and *where was Tim?* She wondered if something had happened between Tim and Susan. She wished more than anything now that she'd had the courage to ask Tim to the dance.

Then, a feeling of sadness set in as she thought about the note she'd written on his birthday card. She was positive she had ruined her chances.

"How's it going?" The voice startled Annette as she swung around. Tim had managed to find her and sat down next to her on the bleachers.

"Tim!" Annette's hand went to her heart and she stifled a smile.

He looked out at the dance floor and sighed. "I guess neither one of us is having a very good time tonight."

Annette didn't know what to say. Susan and Steve were now entwined as another slow dance began. She caught a glimpse of Pete and Penny behind a bunch of other dancers.

"Happy Valentines Day, Annette."

She looked up at him and caught his smile. His green eyes were full of warmth as he gazed at her face. Then he nudged her shoulder with his. "Let's go outside and get some air. Grab your coat."

20

Suspicious Activity

Without a word, Annette stood up and found her coat and purse, then followed Tim as he put on his leather jacket and they headed out of the gymnasium toward the back parking lot. Her heart began to beat faster. The night air was cold and a chilly wind blew her hair as she gathered the collar of her coat around her bare neck.

"Come on, let's get into my car," said Tim. They passed a couple who were walking toward the building as Annette followed Penny's brother around the corner, near the back entrance to the school building. They walked past the band room, where everything looked dark and deserted. Tim led the way to his Chevelle, which was parked away from the rest.

He opened the passenger door and Annette climbed in. Then Tim hurried around to get into the driver's seat. He smiled at her. "Cold?" he asked.

"Yes." Annette hugged herself. There was a faint odor of perfume, probably lingering from Susan's presence earlier.

Tim started the engine up, then said, "It should be warm in a minute or two." He sat back against the seat and sighed. "Kind of a bummer dance, wasn't it?" Before she could reply, he asked, "How come my sister was hogging Pete out on the dance floor?"

Even though it was dark in the car, she could see that Tim was studying her carefully and she felt self-conscious all of a sudden. "It's complicated," she murmured.

"What's wrong?" asked Tim. "Did you guys have a fight or something?"

"No," said Annette. She was reluctant to explain the situation, so instead she said, "What happened to you and Susan?"

Tim chuckled and shook his head slowly. "I guess she found a better offer. I saw her trying to hit on your brother Terry."

Annette broke out giggling as the tension broke between them. "Yes, you should have seen Debbie Kelton yanking him away from her." Then they both laughed. Annette sighed and said, "I guess Pete and I broke up."

"Mmm. I see," said Tim. There was a long silence, and then he sighed again and said, "This is a good time for us to have a talk."

Annette immediately grew worried. "Okay," she finally said after a long pause. "What do you wanna talk about?"

"I've put this off long enough," Tim said gently.

"What?" Annette was suddenly afraid of what he might say.

"I think you know already ... don't you?"

Annette hung her head and stared into her lap. "It's ... it's about the birthday card, isn't it?" *Oh, here it comes,* she thought. *He must hate me.*

"Partly," said Tim. "What you wrote ..."

Then Annette erupted in protest. "Tim! I'm sorry. I was out of bounds ... and I didn't mean to offend you." He stared at her in surprise, but she couldn't hold back. "Honestly, the last thing I wanted was to push you away." She felt like she was going to cry.

"Who said anything about your being out of bounds?"

asked Tim.

"Well, wasn't I?" She dared to look at his face in the dimness of the dashboard lighting. He peered into her eyes.

"Look, Annette ... you're not like any other girl I've known. I feel I can talk to you about anything. But it seems like in the last couple of weeks, you've been ... well, avoiding me."

"No, Tim ..." She shook her head slowly.

"Are you afraid of me?" he asked. When she didn't answer right away, Tim continued, "Hey, I know I'm 18 now, and you're only 15 ... maybe you're afraid I'll take advantage of you." Then he added, "I want you to know, I'll never do anything to hurt you." After a pause, he said, "Annette, if you really didn't mean what you wrote on my card, just admit it. Tell me right here and now ... and I'll understand. And I'll let you go on with your ... *life*." His voice faltered on that last word.

"Tim," she said as her heart swelled with emotion, "I meant every single word I wrote. You've got to know ... I like you so much ... and what's more, I wanted to invite you to the Valentines Dance, but I was afraid Pete's feelings would be hurt. I knew he and Penny liked each other, but she kept insisting that *I* ask him. Then I was afraid if I *did* ask you, you wouldn't want to go to the dance with a ... *sophomore*." At that point, Annette couldn't hold back her tears any longer and she angrily began to wipe at her eyes.

Tim reached his arm out behind Annette and drew her closer to him. "Please don't cry," he said. But even as she tried to lean toward him, the stick shift console blocked the way. "This isn't exactly comfortable, is it?" he commented.

Annette looked into his face with her tear-stained cheeks and laughed. "Not really."

He gently reached over and drew her head against his shoulder, in spite of the stick shift. "Let me just hold you awhile. Do you mind?"

Tim's fingers tousled her hair as they sat as close as the console would let them. It felt so good to be there beside the boy she cared most about, and together they stared out the windshield at the back of the school building, basking in the warmth from the car's heater and the relief of knowing they were alone together.

Suddenly, some movement startled Annette. She jerked up from her position and said, "Someone's out there."

"What?" Tim had been resting his eyes while playing with her hair and now leaned toward the window. "What did you see?"

Annette looked around and then they saw a male figure sneaking around the corner of the school building from the direction of the football field. The individual was too far away for her to recognize who it was, but Tim had seen him too. They watched as the person tried the door that led into the band room, which was locked. He then stepped away and looked in both directions and retreated behind the corner of the building.

"It doesn't look like he's up to any good," said Tim.

"What should we do?" asked Annette.

"Let's wait a minute," he replied. They continued to watch, and then they saw two male figures at the corner of the building, discussing something. Both disappeared around the corner again, and this time Tim shut off the car engine. Annette moved back against her seat, wondering what he was going to do.

"I'm going to check this out," said Tim. "Annette, you wait here." He started to open his door.

"Tim, I don't think that's a good idea," she said.

"Don't worry, I'm not going to do anything foolish."

He carefully stepped out of the car and then casually walked over to the locked door to the band room while Annette sat in the car, worried and excited. Tim stood at the locked door for a few seconds, then started toward the side of the building where they had last seen the two guys.

When he disappeared from her view, she couldn't stand the suspense a moment longer and opened the car door and climbed out.

B y the time they got to the river bank, Joe was so ill, he was delirious. It was afternoon, hot and humid, and the two Vietnamese guides held Joe up while Lloyd Lovingood disappeared into the foliage beside the Hué River. Joe knew he was hallucinating. Strange images came into his head and he was afraid his brain was cooking. "Ruth … where are the kids?" he panted.

The guides could only scowl and try to keep him quiet. Finally, after a short time, Lloyd returned and was excited. He spoke to his guides in their language, and then together they carried Joe to the water's edge. A boat was several yards out from shore, and Joe was positive he must be dreaming … but he recognized the gray hull of what he recognized as a U.S. Navy patrol boat recon.

As the craft approached shore, he saw four sailors on board dressed in O.D. greens with helmets. The skipper stood at the wheel of the boat with a M-16 rifle in one of his hands. He saw on board the PBR two men—gunners—who came to the side of the craft as it bobbed alongside the swampy shore. Joe fell in and out of consciousness, but then he felt his body being lifted by the two men onto the craft. At that point, Lloyd and the two Vietnamese men had vanished from sight. Joe was laid on the floor of the boat, and at that moment he passed out.

A nnette approached the school building, shivering in the wintry night air. She could hear faint rock and roll music booming from inside the gym on the opposite side. Tim had not returned and she was worried.

She decided to check things out and walked to the corner where she had last seen the two individuals, as well as Tim following them. No one was in sight, so she continued on along that side of the building, which contained storage bins for waste and a shed that housed either a generator or the school's heating system. It hummed.

When she heard human voices, she quickly hid herself behind one of the little sheds and waited. Soon two young men came into sight, both wearing jackets, caps and gloves. They hesitated only ten feet from her and she overheard their conversation.

"Let's get out of here," one of the young men was saying. "I don't want to do this." He sounded anxious.

The other man, obviously a little older, said, "Unless we create a diversion, how're we gonna get the animals out of the county? B.J., you know the sheriff's got road blocks set up."

Annette almost gasped. *B.J.?* Could it be ... Bruce Lupenski, Mrs. Pruett's nephew?

"You promised me this will be the last haul," said B.J. "I'm in enough trouble as it is."

"You're an idiot. Why'd you lose that stupid medal at that farmhouse?"

"Dang it, Waldo, how the hell was I s'posed to know the chain had broken?"

"Okay, kid. Here's what I want you to do," said Waldo, pulling something out of a knapsack. He handed something to B.J.

"You go around and sneak into the gym. There's a dance going on, by the sounds of it."

"What if somebody sees me?" asked B.J.

Waldo sneered in reply. "Nobody will notice if you act normal instead of a bungling idiot. Pretend you're a student ... maybe you're there to pick up your sister or something. Figure it out!"

"Okay … then what?" asked B.J.

Waldo and B.J. had their backs to Annette, so she couldn't watch, but they were mumbling to each other, and then she heard Waldo say, "Find a dark classroom and empty the contents of the vial into a waste basket that has a lot of paper in it. Then all you have to do is light the match and leave. But you'd better get out of there before the smoke alarms go off in the school."

B.J. groaned. "Then what, Waldo?"

"Then meet me at the truck and trailer. I have the rig parked in back of the elementary school. Know where that is?"

"Yup," said B.J. "But how can you be sure they're not gonna catch us?"

"Because, lame brain, all the pigs in this cow town are gonna be *here* at the high school, putting out the fire! Now get goin'."

B.J. walked off toward the gymnasium entrance, where the dance was going on, and the older fellow named Waldo turned and headed back in the direction of the parking lot.

Annette knew she had to do something … and fast! She was quite sure that B.J. and Waldo were the livestock rustlers from the conversation she'd overheard. So, B.J., or Bruce, *had* been involved and obviously had been the one to drop the county fair medallion on her property two nights ago. She wanted to run after B.J. and stop him before he could commit arson and endanger all her schoolmates' lives. But her first concern was for Tim—where was he?

Suddenly she heard yelling. She turned in the direction Waldo had taken. Two figures struggled in the dark, next to the school building where the band room was located. Tim was in combat with the man named Waldo, who struck the teen-ager, who fell to the ground.

"Tim!" Annette cried out in alarm. At once, Waldo took off toward the parking lot. Annette ran over to Penny's brother and knelt down beside him as he groveled and groaned. "Tim, are you okay?"

Tim was obviously in pain, but he wasn't knocked out. He held the side of his head as he attempted to get to his feet. "Annette … you could have gotten hurt. Why didn't you stay in the car?"

"Tim! We've got to stop B.J."

"Who's B.J.?" asked Tim, who was finally able to stand, but was wobbly on his feet.

"Bruce Lupenski, one of the rustlers," said Annette, and she quickly told him about the conversation she had just overheard and how Bruce was on his way into the gym now to start the fire.

"We've got to alert the police," said Tim. "Come on."

"*Not so fast.*" A deep, husky voice called out to them from the shadows, and then B.J. and another, larger man stepped out and confronted Annette and Tim. The other man was tall and heavy with a black beard and wore a stocking hat. In front of him he held a large switchblade and thrust it toward them.

B.J. said in an agitated voice, "She's the one got me into trouble."

"Well, she's gonna be no trouble from now on," snarled the large man as he closed the distance between them.

Annette could see that she and Tim were trapped. B.J. grabbed her arm and held her while the other man grabbed Tim and wielded the blade close to his neck.

"What're we gonna do with 'em, Zeke?' asked B.J., who was panting.

"Over there," Zeke said, indicating the band room section of the school. The two men forced Annette and Tim over to the wall and then Zeke said to B.J., "Break that window." He grabbed hold of Annette with his other hand while B.J. picked up a brick from a pile of refuse and hurled it.

The glass smashed and bits of it shattered. "Now get

inside," Zeke ordered. "You first, B.J."

B.J. scrambled up and through the window's opening.

"You next," Zeke ordered, glaring at Annette. She struggled, but he tightened his grip and shoved her over to the window.

"Do as he says, Annette," Tim told her with a groan.

Relenting, Annette climbed up to where B.J. reached through and pulled her inside. She was aware of the shards of glass everywhere and tried not to cut herself on any of them.

"You next!" Zeke ordered Tim, who scrambled up and fell into the room. Zeke followed behind him, amazingly agile for his great size. "Now get them into those little closets," he told B.J.

Annette and Tim saw that Zeke meant one of the practice rooms that were in the band room. At knife point, they were herded inside the nearest one. The moment the door closed, Tim lunged toward it, trying to get it open. Zeke laughed from outside. He was holding the doorknob so it wouldn't turn.

Soon they could hear a heavy table or some cabinet being pushed toward the practice room. Tim struggled with the doorknob, but already the furniture was preventing them from getting out.

"Now what?" they heard B.J. ask.

Zeke grew angry. "Waldo gave you the lighter? Well, *light it off!*"

"Here? Now?" cried B.J.

Zeke hurled a series of expletives at B.J. and then their voices trailed away into silence. In the dark practice room, Annette groped for Tim, and when she felt him he clutched her and they held each other. "Tim, they've started the fire in the band room," Annette whimpered.

"I'm afraid so," he said with a tremor in his voice.

Annette clung to him. She had never been so scared in her life.

21

Fire!

Penny came out of the restroom and looked around at the crowd. She hadn't seen Annette in at least half an hour. Pete was resting on the bleachers, visiting with one of his chums, and Penny saw Susan Reed still hanging out with Steve Newton, so she walked over to them. As soon as they saw her, both of them stopped and stared.

"Uh … *Penny!*" Steve looked as if he were about to make an excuse, but she abruptly cut him off.

"Have you seen Annette?"

"Who?" asked Susan.

"Annette Vetter," said Steve. "You know Annette?"

"Oh … *her* … Terry's sister."

"No, we haven't seen her," said Steve.

Penny placed her hands on her hips and demanded, "And where is Tim?"

Susan scowled and turned her back on Penny. Steve shrugged and said, "Sorry, Penny. We don't know." He gave her a silly grin, then put his arm around Susan and they strolled away.

With a frustrated sigh, Penny turned around and marched toward the bleachers. Terry and Debbie were lingering nearby, so she stopped and asked them, "Have either of you seen Annette or Tim?"

Debbie's eyes widened. "No!"

Terry, looking concerned, gazed around the room. "The last I saw of them, they were sitting here on the bleachers together … but heck, that was quite a while ago."

Debbie covered her mouth and giggled. "Maybe they went parking."

Penny rolled her eyes. Then Pete stood up and came over. "What's the matter?" he asked.

"Nobody knows where Annette is," Penny explained.

"Or Tim," added Terry.

"Well, they probably went somewhere," said Debbie.

Pete led Penny aside. "If it would make you feel better, we can see if Debbie's right. Get your coat and we'll go check Tim's Chevelle."

"Okay." Penny smiled up at Pete. "Thank you for being so … caring."

They grabbed their coats, then hurried outside to the parking lot. It took them awhile to locate Tim's car because he had parked it so far away, near the band room.

"Nope, they're not here," said Penny, looking around. "How odd. But look, Tim left his keys in the car."

Pete grabbed her arm and pointed toward the school. "Hey … is that smoke I see?"

Penny looked in that direction and they could see smoke pouring out of a window on the inside alley. Before she could say a word, Pete took off running toward the band room and Penny followed him.

"It's coming from inside," cried Penny. "The band room's on fire!"

By now Pete had reached the broken window and an orange glow was visible from the front of the room that led into the back hallway.

"We've got to call the fire department," Penny told him.

"There should be a fire alarm inside," said Pete. He started climbing up into the open window.

"Pete! What are you doing?" she cried. "There's a lot of smoke!"

"Wait here," he told her as he slipped inside. He pulled a handkerchief out of his jacket pocket and covered his mouth, bending low to the floor as he made his way toward the classroom door. Familiar with the band room, he knew a fire alarm was close by that doorway.

As he crossed the room, he suddenly heard cries coming from somewhere nearby. Pete stopped to listen. He heard two people calling out, "Help us! Please! Somebody! Help!"

Pete looked in all directions, but the dark room made it almost impossible to see. By then, Penny had managed to climb in through the broken window and could also hear the cries for help.

"Turn on the light!" Penny called out to Pete.

He managed to get to the light switch, fighting smoke and watching small curls of flame eating the walls in the instrument storage room. Pete flicked on the fluorescent ceiling lights and right away they saw the pile of chairs and the table that had been barricaded outside one of the practice rooms.

"Annette's in there!" screamed Penny, tripping her way over.

Pete got the band room door open, and struggling with the smoke, reached up and pulled the fire alarm. Right away the bell went off throughout the entire school as Pete stumbled his way back into the band room and dodged his way over to help Penny clear away the obstructions.

They could hear Annette inside, pounding on the door, and then Tim's voice rang out, "Hurry!"

Pete was able to finally move the cabinet that was blocking the doorknob, and the moment it was free the door flew open. Annette and Tim practically fell out, freed at last.

"Quick! We've got to get out of here." Pete started coughing.

Penny was choking on the smoke as well, but grabbed hold of Annette, who wouldn't let go of Tim's hand as they stayed low and made their way to the window. Flames had already reached the door to the band room, so there was no escape into the hallway.

One by one, they scrambled through the open window, first Annette, then Penny, Tim and finally Pete. As they got to their feet and were clearing their throats and chests of the awful smoke, they heard fire sirens approaching. Pete ushered them toward the parking lot, where people were flooding out from the dance, frightened and befuddled.

Suddenly, Terry, followed by Debbie, came running toward them. "Annette! Are you okay?" he cried.

"Tim, what happened?" Penny was finally able to speak, but continued to cough.

"Come on, let's get clear of the area," Terry shouted and led their group over to the gathering crowd as two Ravensville fire trucks drove up into the school parking lot, their lights flashing. A rescue truck followed, along with two Ravensville police cars. Red and blue lights were flashing everywhere.

"We're okay … we're fine," Tim reassured everyone, though his voice was husky now from breathing smoke.

"I need to talk to the police right away," Annette demanded. Her tear-stained face was blotched from the dust and the smoke.

Terry heard her and ran over to one of the squad cars. The firemen were bringing the hoses up when a patrolman rushed over to Annette, who was sitting on the curb beside Tim, who had his arm around her.

"Do you know who started the fire?" was the first thing that the policeman asked her.

Annette nodded. "Bruce Lupenski," she said. "And a man named Zeke … and another man named Waldo. They're the livestock rustlers, and they're getting away as we speak!" She then told the story to everyone around her, and the officer took notes, then was joined by another policeman, who got wind of what was happening and returned to the squad car to call in an A.P.B.

"Our school!" a girl was wailing from the parking lot.

"I can't believe this is happening," someone else cried.

Annette and Tim, accompanied by Pete and Penny, Terry and Debbie, walked over to where the fire trucks and patrol cars were parked. An EMT wanted to check them over, especially Tim, who said he had only suffered a few bruises and there was nothing to worry about.

"Annette, I was so worried." Penny was crying as she held Annette's hand.

"It was because of Pete and Penny that you were rescued," said Debbie.

"Yeah, if it hadn't been for them … I hate to even think of it." Terry was close to tears.

Half an hour later, the fire had been extinguished. Fortunately, only the band room had suffered any damage. The fire department had arrived in time to prevent a worse crisis. The crowd finally dispersed as the kids departed, sorry that the Valentines Dance had ended on such a tragic note.

"Let's go home," said Annette, suddenly exhausted.

"I'll drive you," said Tim gently. "Penny? Pete?"

"Terry's taking us," Pete told him, his arm around Tim's sister. They were also taking Debbie home.

"I guess Steve and Susan already left," said Penny.

"Long ago," chuckled Pete.

Annette followed Tim over to the Chevelle and they drove home to Ogden Road, where everything was serene and welcoming. "Whew, what an evening it was," Tim commented as he pulled into the Vetters' driveway. The porch light was still on, Annette noticed. Her mother was probably waiting up for her and Terry.

"It certainly was," she told him with a smile and reached her hand toward him. He took her hand in his and squeezed it, then gazed into her eyes.

"I'll call you in the morning," said Tim.

"Okay. Good night."

"Good night, Annette."

She opened the car door and stepped out. Ginger was barking from the kitchen and the next thing she knew, Mrs. Vetter was standing at the door, watching her.

Annette waved to Tim, then blew him a kiss. As the Chevelle backed down the driveway, Annette hurried up the porch steps, so grateful to have this little home in the country with her mom, Terry and Ruby, Ginger and her cows.

What a lucky girl she was ... and now she was Tim's girl-friend in addition to everything else.

22

Ground Hog Stew

The minute Annette got inside the house, her mother, Uncle Will and Ruby surrounded her with worried expressions. The police had called Mrs. Vetter earlier, letting her know that there had been trouble at school, but Annette was all right.

"What happened to your face?" cried Ruby when she saw the smudges and scratches from the ordeal Annette and Tim had suffered.

"Go upstairs and clean up first," directed Mrs. Vetter. "Then you can come down and tell us what happened."

"Mom, it's not as bad as it looks." Annette examined the palms of both hands, which had been pricked a little by the loose glass from the broken window. "I'm going to survive."

By the time Annette had jumped into the shower and changed into her bathrobe and slippers, Terry arrived home after delivering Debbie, Penny and Pete to their homes. When she came downstairs, Mrs. Vetter and Uncle Will were fixing hot chocolate for everyone. Even though it was rather late, they all sat around the table in the dining room while Annette told them everything that had happened at the school.

Terry filled in the part about Penny being worried and how she and Pete had gone outside to the parking lot, had seen the smoke, and had gone in through the broken window to pull the fire alarm. "And if it hadn't been for them, Annette and Tim might not have been found in time." His voice wavered.

Ruby stood up and went over to throw her arms around Annette. "I'm so glad Pete and Penny got you out of there before the fire spread."

Uncle Will, who usually didn't get too excited about anything, grew angry. "Well, those thugs should be convicted for attempted murder!"

"I certainly hope the police were able to stop them," said Mrs. Vetter. "But I guess we won't know anything until tomorrow."

"Even if the rustlers got away tonight," said Annette, "I'm sure they'll track them down, especially since one of them was Bruce Lupenski."

"Lucy Pruett's nephew," Uncle Will grumbled. "This isn't going to set well with Fred."

After they talked a bit more, Annette grew tired and set her empty mug down on the table. "I am so exhausted." She yawned, then stretched.

"I think we all need to get to bed," said Mrs. Vetter. She pushed her chair back and started gathering the empty mugs to take to the kitchen sink.

Later, while Annette was brushing out her damp hair in the bedroom, Ruby changed into her pajamas and said, "That's really groovy about you and Tim." She smiled.

Annette looked at her sister in the mirror and sighed. "Yes, I can still hardly believe it." Then she set the brush down on the dresser. "Oh, I'm too tired to set my hair tonight."

When they finally got settled under the covers and Annette turned off the bedside lamp, Ruby rolled over onto her side and almost instantly fell asleep. Annette prayed there would be no nightmares tonight.

Joe came to inside a large room aboard a U.S. Navy vessel. He soon realized he was in their sick bay and an IV was in his arm. It was warm and sterile in the room. He had no idea how long he had been out, but he had been cleaned up and medicated. He guessed the patrol boat had transported him to this ship. Crew took turns caring for him and an officer showed up once he was awake, to debrief him.

"Good morning," the lieutenant greeted him as he pulled up a stool beside Joe's cot. "I'm Lieutenant Oliver. Your name, please?"

Joe was too weak to sit up, but he wasn't expected to do so. "Dunno," he mumbled. "They call me Joe."

"Joe. Last name? Rank?"

"No last name." Then he added, "Major."

"Air Force?"

"Yes."

"No dog tags on you?" asked the lieutenant.

"The Viet Cong took everything," he explained, almost too tired to talk.

"You were in a prison camp?"

Joe nodded and the lieutenant started writing on a notepad.

"The man who brought you to us … who was he?" asked Lieutenant Oliver.

Joe groaned and looked at the tray next to him, where there was a bottle with water and a straw. Understanding his need, the officer picked up the bottle and held it so that Joe could sip some of the water. Then Joe continued, "Lovingood … Lloyd," he murmured. "He's a Brit."

"He's a smuggler," the lieutenant informed him. "He's wanted."

Joe had figured as much, but the officer didn't seem too worried about it. Lloyd Lovingood had done the right thing in bringing him to the American military.

"What happened to you? Do you remember anything at all?"

"Not much," Joe admitted. "My pilot and I were flying to a base to check on supplies there. I think we were hit by Triple A. We managed to parachute out. We walked for days and then we got captured. I don't know when I lost my memory … but I don't know who I am, or where I come from. All I remember is that Bill called me Major. That's all I remember … Major."

The lieutenant was busy writing and nodding his head. "Do you know the pilot's … Bill's … last name?" he asked.

"Crawford," said Joe. "Bill Crawford … yes, that's the only thing I remember." There was a pause and then he added in a somber voice, "He didn't make it."

Lieutenant Oliver summoned a nearby medic in the room and gave some orders that Joe didn't hear. He had closed his eyes after exerting himself by talking so much to the officer.

He didn't know he had slipped off to sleep until someone nudged him a short while later. Joe opened his eyes to Lieutenant Oliver and another man. "Does Operation Ground Hog mean anything to you?" he asked Joe.

Ground Hog! Joe's brain suddenly came alive with a flash of familiarity. With wide eyes, he stared up at the men and said, "Yes … yes, it does. Ground Hog was our secret mission. It's also … it's also my birthday. Ground Hog Day."

The two men consulted again so that Joe couldn't hear, and then the lieutenant dismissed the other man and smiled at Joe. "Congratulations," he said. "I believe we have a positive identity on you."

Joe stared up at the lieutenant, relieved but so fatigued. "What's wrong with me? Why am I in sick bay?" he asked.

"You have dysentery," said Lieutenant Oliver. "But you're going to be fine, Bob."

"Bob?" Joe repeated, looking the lieutenant in the eye.

"My name is … Bob?"

"Major Robert Foley," replied the lieutenant. "You were listed as M.I.A. But now, rest assured … you are on your way home."

The next morning Annette woke up, feeling refreshed. Ginger shook himself as he got up off the floor. She dressed quickly, then went downstairs to put on her boots and farm coat, so she could go out to milk the cows. Everyone else in the house was still asleep.

But just before she went out the door, Uncle Will emerged from the living room, wearing his tan bathrobe and moccasins. "Good morning," he said to Annette as he scratched his disheveled white hair.

"Hi, Uncle Will."

"I'm going to make coffee," he said as he headed for the cupboard.

Annette smiled, then she and the collie went out into the crisp morning air. The sun was just starting to come up in the east, across the road. This morning as she walked to the barn, she had a lift in her step and a song in her heart, thinking about last night when she and Tim had sat in the car and had their talk. As she went about her routine of milking, she went over every detail, every word they had exchanged, and especially the wonderful part about their holding each other.

Her thoughts then turned to Penny, probably still asleep right now in her bedroom at the Duncan farm. Was Penny having a happy dream about Pete Randt? Now she was so glad the evening had ended the way it did, with Pete and Penny together … and it was interesting how Penny's date, Steve Newton, and Tim's date, Susan Reed, had come together, which had left Annette and Tim to work out their differences. How perfect the world seemed, now that Tim Duncan was her proclaimed boyfriend!

Then, Annette thought about all the trouble resulting from the rustlers. Those three—Waldo, Bruce or B.J., and Zeke—had caused a lot of harm in the county. Now they had burned up the band room at the high school, and she and Tim had almost lost their lives! She knew they weren't truly safe until those three criminals were behind bars.

When Annette came back into the house with a carton of eight still-warm eggs from the hen house, Uncle Will was sitting at the kitchen table, drinking his coffee, and Mrs. Vetter, who had already dressed, came downstairs to greet them.

"Police just called," Uncle Will announced, stirring fresh cream and sugar into his coffee cup.

"Yes, I heard the phone ring," said Mrs. Vetter as she went to the cupboard to get her cup.

"What did they say?" Annette asked eagerly as she hung up her coat and joined them.

"That Lupenski kid turned himself in," said Uncle Will. "He also gave the police information on the other two. One was a cousin of his from Duluth."

"Which one?" asked Annette. "Zeke or Waldo?"

"It was Waldo," said Uncle Will. "Anyway, they were able to arrest the cousin, and they're going to get the ring-leader, Zeke. He was the brains of the outfit, apparently. He had the truck and trailer and was connected to black-market sales in three states."

"Good grief," remarked Mrs. Vetter. She poured herself some coffee, then came to sit down at the table. Annette took a seat as well.

"Anyway, there's a good chance some of the farmers will get their animals back."

"Well, I hope the Randts get their heifers back," said Annette, "and Fred his horses. I still can't believe his wife's nephew aided and abetted in stealing Fred's horses."

"That's probably the reason they used Bruce," said Uncle

Will. "He knew a lot about the Pruetts' neighbors and it was said that he worked at several of the farms in the area, so he had inside information."

Soon Terry and Ruby came downstairs and Mrs. Vetter decided to whip up a batch of blueberry pancakes. Everyone cheered.

While they were eating and discussing their plans for the day, the phone rang. Annette wiped some blueberry juice off her mouth and went to pick up the phone. "Hello."

"Annette." It was Tim. "How are you this morning?"

"Oh, Tim. I'm fine. How are you?"

Aware that her family was listening, Annette tried to calm herself, but just the sound of his voice was sending chills throughout her body. He told her the police had called him that morning as well, and they were on their way to pick up the two older criminals. "That guy, B.J., is already in jail," said Tim.

"Thank goodness." Annette breathed a sigh of relief. "Is Penny up yet?"

"No, she's still sound asleep," said Tim. "Hey, I have an idea. I've got some free time this afternoon. How about if I come over and take you out for your first driving lesson?"

"Really?" Annette grinned. "I'd love that."

"Good. I'll come by about two."

After she hung up, Annette returned to the table with a smile on her face.

"I was just telling Uncle Will about my dream this morning," Ruby said to Annette. "Do you want to hear it?"

Annette snapped out of her euphoria and nodded her head. "Yes, Ruby. Go ahead and tell me. What was your dream about?"

Both Terry and Mrs. Vetter were smiling, so Annette knew it must have been a good dream.

Ruby's blue eyes sparkled as she said, "I had another

dream about my dad."

"Yeah?" encouraged Annette, reaching for her glass of milk.

"He was walking through a really scary field and when he got to the water, there was a big ship. Then he was inside the ship and somebody gave him a bowl of ground hog stew."

Annette and Terry laughed out loud.

Ruby blinked her eyes. "I know that doesn't make sense. And then they told him it was time for him to go home." She grew excited. "Annette, I just *know* that my dad is on his way home right now!"

Uncle Will shot a look of warning in Annette's direction. She knew better than to burst Ruby's bubble of hope. "Oh Ruby, that's wonderful news," said Annette. "I sure hope you are right."

"I *am* right," said Ruby.

Everyone laughed then, and Mrs. Vetter got up to take the last batch of pancakes off the cast iron griddle on the stove.

Annette sat back and watched the other three people at the dining table. How happy everyone was this morning. They were truly a family, and ... who knew? Perhaps Ruby wanted her father to be alive so badly that maybe he really *was* coming home.

Time would tell.

THE END

About the Author

Ann Carol Ulrich started writing about Annette Vetter when she was 15, growing up in the '60s.

The Ground Hog Mystery is the sixth in her Annette Vetter series.

A native of Wisconsin, Ms. Ulrich has lived in Michigan, Ohio, Washington and Oregon, but has spent most of her life in Colorado. She currently is at home in Cedaredge, Colorado.

Visit her Author Website at **AnnUlrichMiller.com**, and Annette invites you to check her out on Facebook (*under Annette Vetter, of course*).

The Annette Vetter Adventure Series

The Mystery at Hickory Hill (August 1968) takes place in the Cochetopa Hills of Colorado when Annette and Penny take a vacation out West before school starts.

The Secret of the Green Paint (September 1968) starts on the first day of school, when Annette makes a new friend in her Art class and also notices that new boy who lives on the farm down the road.

The Pouting Pumpkin Mystery (October 1968) celebrates Homecoming at Ravensville High, with a Halloween theme that involves HAM radio.

The Legend of the Lantern (November 1968) takes place over Thanksgiving weekend, during an early blizzard while Annette and Penny baby-sit for the Randt children while their mom has a new baby.

In the Shadow of the Tower (December 1968) introduces Terry and Ruby into the series, making Christmas a very special holiday for Annette, in addition to a new mystery.

For more information on Annette Vetter books
and others in the Earth Star collection,
visit **www.earthstarpublications.com**

The Ground Hog Mystery
and all of the other *Annette Vetter Adventures*
are also available as eBooks at Amazon Kindle

Pete

Penny

Tim

Annette

Terry

Ruby